THE COUNTRY WILL BRING US NO PEACE

a novel without music by **MATTHIEU SIMARD**
translated by **PABLO STRAUSS**

Coach House Books, Toronto

Coach House Books acknowledges the financial support of the Government
of Canada through the National Translation Program for Book Publishing,
an initiative of the Roadmap for Canada's Official Languages 2013–2019:
Education, Immigration, Communities, for our translation activities. We
are also grateful for generous assistance for our publishing program from
the Canada Council for the Arts and the Ontario Arts Council. Coach House
Books also acknowledges the support of the Government of Canada through
the Canada Book Fund.

LIBRARY AND ARCHIVES CANADA CATALOGUING IN PUBLICATION

Title: The country will bring us no peace / Matthieu Simard ; translated by
Pablo Strauss.
Other titles: Ici, ailleurs. English
Names: Simard, Matthieu, author. | Strauss, Pablo, translator.
Description: Translation of: Ici, ailleurs.
Identifiers: Canadiana (print) 20190141018 | Canadiana (ebook)
20190141913 | ISBN 9781552453933 (SOFTCOVER) | ISBN 9781770566132
(PDF) | ISBN 9781770566125 (EPUB)
Classification: LCC PS8637.I42 I2413 2019 | DDC C843/.6—dc23

The Country Will Bring Us No Peace is available as an ebook: ISBN 978 1 77056
612 5 (EPUB) 978 1 77056 613 5 (PDF)

À Papa
To you I dedicate the first of my books you will never read.

We cannot go to the country
for the country will bring us no peace
— William Carlos Williams,
'Raleigh Was Right'

The silence came down on us like rain one Thursday, and we spent years submerged in it. The birds fell silent and rusty hinges stopped squeaking and no children hollered in the schoolyard. The passenger-side car speaker died; dead leaves ceased to rustle in the wind. Just silence. That was three years ago, far from here.

We've weathered hundreds of storms since then. And each time she's been there to tap me on the shoulder and remind me of the days before.

Forty years from now there will be nothing left of us. Our memory and the photographs and the recollections of those who disappeared will all be gone, like the notes from a cello in the ruins of an old house.

Marie stares at the wall. The spectre of a migraine is fluttering in her grey eyes. Her nails pierce the cardboard box she's sitting on, and a heartbeat is audible. It might be hers, it might be mine. A small living room. Dirty walls. A low-hanging sun. And silence.

The truck just pulled out of the unpaved alley. Dozens of boxes are piled at the back of the room, and three others sit in front of me. Marie's gaze turns to the black case leaning against the wall. She rubs her temple, makes a weak attempt to hide the grimace as her elbow stutters. I know by heart what she's about to do and the conversation we're about to have. Our cello scene is well-rehearsed, though we've yet to find the right ending or perfect melody. She gets up, drags her feet over to the case, opens it, pulls out her Josef Klotz, slides another box over, and sits down, poised to begin a performance that will never happen. She takes a deep breath, sets the horsehair down on the instrument's strings, sighs, and then slouches down in disappointment.

'Every single time …'

'Don't worry.'

'I don't know why I keep it around.' She puts away the instrument, closes the case. Her finger massages her temple.

'Did you take your –'

'Three. Makes no difference, though.'

She has the most beautiful eyes in the world, the colour of boreal mist, and a pain I can never allay. The floor creaks under my feet. I pick her coat up off the ground. Though it's almost summer, the evenings are cool here in the country.

'We need to celebrate.'

'Yeah. I guess.'

Celebrate that we've made it here, and all the possibilities of the weeks ahead. Four months of running without moving forward, a river with no current, our lacerated memories. Our summer, here.

~

I put my cello down in a corner of the room. If I could, I would have shoved it right into the wall until it disappeared from sight. Simon handed me my coat and we went out. Stifling humidity, heavy clouds, a visible film of dust hovering above the road.

The only bar in town is down that road, in front of a wall of evergreens that separates the rest of the solar system from this relative civilization. The sign in the window is far from inviting. Nor is the rusty pickup on the lawn in front. Without discussion, we hesitate a moment in front of the wooden door, immobilized by the fear of our first time out for drinks here – the time that will make or break our chances of ever being at home in this town. We take a deep breath, then another, and in we go.

It's the kind of roadhouse you see here and there, maybe everywhere, with a floor still marked by the boots of some Jim and littered with some Randy's cigarette butts. The kind of place that still smells like the working guys who drank here years ago. Three drinkers sit at three different tables, staring now at the wall, now into space. Big bottles of Labatt 50 on the bar. A thousand stains from past drinks on our table. The creak of my chair every time I move. The waitress's smile.

'Radio's busted. Fisher's supposed to fix it, but, you know, between this and that … '

Her name is Linda, and she has fair skin and a red mane. We order two big 50s, hoping to expunge our big-city attitude through hearty swigs of local swill. While we take our first sips, and then our twelfth, and then our thirtieth, we have time to acclimate to the thick patch of fog we've unwittingly moved into. We're hazily celebrating our new beginning here, at the opposite end of the spectrum of our usual fresh starts.

We don't talk. From time to time Simon looks at me, and I notice how good he looks. I'd give him a kiss, but I fear my creaking chair will attract attention, so I settle for taking his hand. After each sip his eyes turn to the door, as if he's expecting someone, but it never opens. Another sip. We hold hands in silence, neither one of us daring to admit we're terrified that coming here was a mistake.

An unkempt man in his early forties puts a hand on my arm. It took him an hour to screw up his courage. I knew he'd come talk to us sooner or later, as his furtive glances turned into lingering stares. Whenever we weren't looking, his chair crept an inch closer to us. His hand is stuck on my forearm. Simon lets go of my fingers.

'You bought the old guy's house?'

'The one on the corner, yeah.'

'He would have liked you.'

'The previous owner?'

'He used to like the pretty ladies too. Before he lost his marbles.'

'That so?'

'The hot water heater has to be changed.'

'I don't … We didn't … '

'I can do it for you. I work at the garage, but I can do whatever you guys need. I'm Fisher. Everyone calls me Fisher. I'm from here. If you got any questions, I'm here.'

'Okay.'

'Do you have any?'

'Questions? Well … '

'The upstairs toilet's new. I put her in for the old guy. To pay back some money I owed him. It leaks a little, just give the handle a shake now and then.'

His eyes are locked on me. I try to back away before he notices, but the creak of the chair rings out through the bar. He leans a little closer toward me. I wonder if he's trying to make me uncomfortable. Simon doesn't seem to notice Fisher's patient advance. We take another sip. Country nights are cool; guys who work at the gas station aren't shy; Simon seems to be elsewhere; the bar door stays closed.

'What did you guys come here for? No one comes to live here anymore … '

'We were looking for somewhere quiet.'

'Quiet, huh … Well, there's nothing going on here, that's for sure. Everyone's moving away … '

'And the house was such a good deal.'

'I'll give you a deal on the tank.'

'We're not hard up for money. That's not what I meant. We didn't know – '

'I don't charge much anyway.'

'All we want is to – '

'Since the factory closed down … There's nothing to do … Yeah, since the factory closed. And it's even worse since they put in the antenna.'

'The antenna?'

'Look, this is a quiet town. A nice, quiet town.'

'Okay.'

'You're gonna like it here.'

'Okay.'

'I won't take up any more of your time. And welcome to town. The garage is over there, you can't miss it. There's a big sign. It don't light up anymore. But we're not open at night anyway.'

For the first time, Fisher turns his eyes away from me and looks at Simon.

'You got a pretty wife, man.'

Simon shoots him a polite smile. It's been months since he said it to me, and he knows it. Months without a compliment. And months have passed since I complimented him as well. I shouldn't have let that happen. I feel bad. I look down at my feet. Fisher leans in toward me, and I don't even back away. I should have. He kisses me, on the tips of my lips at first. I don't move. I want to push him away but somehow can't. I close my eyes and he pushes harder, our tongues touch, and then he gets up and walks out, without a word to red-haired, fair-skinned Linda.

Simon stares at his beer. He doesn't even seem mad at me. 'Should we go home?'

Forty years from now, no one will remember this kiss, or this night, or this bar and the infinite emptiness that fills it. Or our house. Or here.

∼

We've barely spoken since Fisher kissed Marie. A few words about the sand from the previous winter still sprinkled over the asphalt. Something about the moon shining through the cloud cover. A sentence or two about the closed-down, boarded-up school.

The master bedroom floor has a pronounced slope, and we have to find little pieces of wood to shim the bedposts. Marie lets her clothing drop where it falls and slips naked under the sole blanket we found in the box marked 'Bedroom closet.' I climb in with her and warm my body against hers. We make love because that's what we have to do.

For a short while I imagined that by coming here we could find refuge in a cocoon of forest, burn the bedsheets with our body heat. We'd rekindle the passion of our early days, nine years ago, almost ten. But it's been years since such passions rocked our bodies. If we still manage to lie intertwined nearly every night, we owe it mainly to the old queen-sized mattress we bought on clearance, such a long time ago. The dip in the centre tells the story of how close we used to be and pushes us toward one another even when we don't think about it.

'About time for a new mattress, hey?'

'No.'

We flat-out refuse to get a new one, scared of seeing two separate dips take form. The sorrow would overwhelm us. We're afraid of ending up as isolated as the individually wrapped pocket coils of our new mattress.

Marie covers up her breasts, as if I were a stranger. Her hand is shaking. I catch my breath.

At this point we don't know that we're going to be the 'murder-suicide' couple. An episode of domestic violence that will briefly make the news and have everyone shaken up for about five minutes, before they forget all about it the moment they turn off their TVs because it's getting late and it's time to go to bed. No one wants to be exhausted the next day. Fisher will say he didn't see it coming, and the Lavoies will say, 'They seemed like such nice people.' Alice won't say a single word. And the blood from our veins will seep into the cracks in the floor of this old house we just bought.

But it's also possible that we knew, even then. That it's been in us for years, just waiting to find the right place, the tiniest of sparks, the correct tool. We came here so as to no longer be there, and we aren't leaving.

Marie sighs.

'We'll be all right here.' She says these words without an inkling of a smile.

Marie blinks. Buffeted by the wind that has kicked up, the window groans. She goes to sleep. I watch her eyelids flutter for a while. My first night here will be a long one. The window's lamentations, the smell of here, my dread of the days ahead. I'll spend hours tossing and turning without waking Marie. And sometimes, when I stare at her lips, I'll think of Fisher.

I'd promised Marie a home-cooked breakfast in the comfort of our boxes, but in the little market the egg shelf is bare. While Marie hangs back next to the tinned fruit salad, I approach the man with white hair and concave shoulders standing behind the till. He smiles.

'You're out of eggs?'

'Yup. Chicken too.'

'Good to know. I wasn't looking for chicken, though.'

'I'm also running low on artichoke hearts. You want some?'

'Not really, no. I was really looking for eggs.'

'You know, sometimes whole weeks go by with no eggs at all, but four cases of bacon. And sometimes it's the other way around. Know why?'

'Nope.'

'Me neither. Honestly, I have no idea what I'm doing here. When Big Bert left us, a few years ago, I took over the grocery store. Because someone had to do it. But I never really understood how it works. And there just weren't as many customers, with so many people leaving, and just a few newcomers like yourselves. But at the same time, you ask me, it's not such a big deal if we lose a few. Take Big Bert, for example – '

'Did he pass away?'

'Something like that. But if you ask me, it's no great loss.'

'Really?'

'Yup. No great loss.'

'Uhh … okay … But what I was really wondering is if you had any eggs. Maybe in the back?'

Marie has joined me by the time the reluctant apprentice grocer confirms that there will be no bacon and eggs for us today. With a shrug, I invite Marie to follow me out of the store. As we're opening the door to leave, the grocer has a few more words for us.

'If it's breakfast you're after, there's always the restaurant on the other side of town. Across from the gas station.'

'The bar? We went yesterday. Didn't especially love it.'

'No, the bar is way over across town. I'm talking about the restaurant, over there. The eggs are nothing to write home about. But it's the only place to eat around here … I mean, the best thing for you guys would probably be to get in with Mrs. Lavoie. I hear she makes good French toast. She's three houses over, on the other side of the church.'

'I think we'll try the restaurant.'

'Say hi to Madeleine for me. The real pretty one. The waitress.'

❧

'The Sexiest Waitresses,' promises the sign outside the restaurant, but that's not why we're here. The glass door is covered with posters for events long past. Neil Diamond Tribute, February 2; Valentine's Day Party, February 12. With her hand still on the doorknob, Marie takes a minute to read a few of these, because they're funny, she says, while I stare at the garage across the street, where Fisher is filling up a Ford Mustang. He waves at me with his free hand. Flashes me a genuine smile. I don't smile back.

The burgundy leatherette booths crackle under our asses, and when a woman in her fifties comes over with menus, I'm happy to see she's dressed from head to toe. Marie's disappointed.

She'd been hoping for another outlandish memory to dissect later. *Remember that waitress on our first morning there? Remember how we laughed?*

At ten o'clock on a Tuesday morning we have the dining room to ourselves. People must be working, or sleeping, or driving right through this place. Maybe they've simply ceased to exist. A car rips through town at eighty miles an hour, and the glass door rattles, and a little cloud of dust is kicked up outside. That's all.

'Don't you guys have a speed limit?'

'The police stopped coming around, and people eventually figured it out. But even when they did come, it didn't change much. They'd write a ticket or two, up at the curve there. Now they don't bother. They've got a new spot, twelve miles over that way.'

Marie still hasn't looked at the menu. There's eggs and bacon and potatoes, just like everywhere else. Beans and sausages. A Wednesday special. It's not Wednesday.

'Made up your minds?'

'Not yet, no.'

'I'll give you a few more minutes. How about a nice cup of coffee?'

'And an orange juice too.'

'Make it two,' says Marie. 'And can I ask you a question?'

'Sure, honey.'

'You aren't … uhhh …?'

The waitress smiles, and grabs the breasts jutting out under her light-blue shirt.

'You saying I'm not sexy?'

Marie looks down. 'That's not … That's not what I meant.'

The waitress guffaws. 'Just messing with you, honey. You're

not the first one to ask. No, we used to work in sexy little outfits. Stopped doing that when the Lavoies had their first little one. Just never got around to taking down the sign. You have any idea what it costs to take down a sign like that?'

'No.'

'I'll be right back with your coffees.'

She'll forget our orange juice, and we won't feel like reminding her. We weren't thirsty anyway. They were out of cream, but there was milk and plenty of sugar, and we ordered eggs. Scrambled for Marie, over easy for me.

'Where you folks headed anyway?' the waitress asks as she sets down our food.

'Nowhere. We just moved here. We live just over –'

'You're the ones who bought the old guy's house!'

'Yeah –'

'Oh, that's great! Welcome to town! I'm Madeleine!'

She lays a hand on Marie's shoulder, which makes Marie jump. I look away. She looks proudly at our plates and adds a few drops of coffee to our already full cups.

'Tell you what – I'll charge you for the Wednesday special.'

The grocer was right: the eggs are nothing to write home about, and the same goes for everything else on our plates. But we're hungry, and with full stomachs and nascent smiles, we just may be experiencing one of those moments Marie so yearns for: a future memory, the start of something beautiful.

Madeleine has just placed our bill down on the corner of the table when a family barges in like they own the place. At the sight of this foursome, the waitress jumps for joy, and that little extra drop in my coffee cup spills onto the paper placemat. Marie knows that irks me.

'Anne! This is the couple that bought the old guy's house!'

The Lavoies sit down next to us. Handshakes, forced smiles, a silence that floats in the air after every question. The Lavoies speak loudly and enunciate clearly. They invite us over for a swim, they have a pool. Though I'm not sure I have a bathing suit, and Marie doesn't know if hers still fits, we say yes nonetheless. We'll go for a dip next week, or later in August when the heat wave comes.

The kids are colouring: a robot for her, a rocket for him. Marie taps her foot. Three months later, nursing warm beers around the pool, we'll be privy to every last detail of the Lavoies' lives. The eldest child's teacher's praise, Christian's fling while he worked on a film set, the youngest one's recurring colds, the reasons Anne-Benedict no longer uses the second part of her name. We won't reciprocate by telling them anything meaningful about ourselves.

Today, against our will, we'll get the highlights. Just when we think we can slide out of our booth and get away, they'll block our retreat with a chorus of voices.

'You know, we don't live here all the time. It's our summer place. We just come on weekends, through June. Then we're here for the rest of the summer. What about you guys?'

'We're going to live here. We sold our house in the city. To live here full-time.'

'Aren't you going to miss the city?'

Marie looked at me, then looked down.

'Doubt it.' What I don't doubt for a moment is that we'll hate the Lavoies, and that Marie will hide it better than I will.

It's been too long since we put Madeleine's tip down on the table, and instead of listening to the Lavoies bragging about their perfect life, I redo the math: 15 per cent isn't much. I mean, she gave us the Wednesday special on a Tuesday. Maybe 18 per cent is more in order. And then Madeleine was so helpful, and our coffees were kept topped up and would stay topped up until the end of time if we so chose. And all those smiles – they weren't even forced. Anne-Benedict is still prattling on about a mortgage, or maybe a snowmobile. Marie is picking at the nail on her right little finger with her left index.

I'm not sure I could ever grow to like their little brats. Six-year-old Patrick is managing to colour in his rocket without ever really going outside the lines. Delphine, four, is slightly less meticulous; she's making little robotic beeps as she scribbles happily away. Red crayon. Yellow crayon. Tiny fingers tearing at the paper wrapper around the crayons. The little guy's broken fingernail. The stain on the young girl's sleeve.

They seem sad. Maybe they're just concentrating, or tired, but I feel like kids cooped up with no one but their parents for such long stretches of time can't really be happy. I feel sorry for them. The coffee on the placemat starts to dry, and I rudely interrupt Anne-Benedict in the middle of her discourse on the health benefits of herbal tea.

'Are they … the only kids in town?'

'Uhh … yeah,' she says. 'But like I was telling Marie – '

'It'll be a long summer!'

'They're real little nature lovers!'

Marie looks at me as if I've saved her life by speaking up. Her hero, offering an exit from that conversation – she doesn't have anything against camomile tea, but when she hears 'the optimal temperature to release the flavour pigments,' a line has been crossed.

'Don't mind him, he can be a little abrupt … And we were cold in the house last night. It makes him grumpy.'

I nod in agreement and pretend to feel bad. We stand up and say that we really have to go unpack some boxes.

～

The wind is blowing like it does in westerns, and we're covered in the dust enveloping the village. With her hair over her eyes and her eyebrows scrunched up, Marie is standing still, although we've barely started our walk to the old guy's house, which is our house now. She leans over and pulls off a sandal, gives it a shake. A stone falls out. It takes a fraction of a second, just long enough to glance over at the gas station across the street.

'Wait a minute … '

I cross the street, dragging my feet, kicking the tiny rubble that has gathered a little farther along the yellow line. With each step, the memory of the previous night's kiss returns. The service station is empty, Fisher nowhere to be found. I go into the little store and up to the counter. On the back wall, behind quarts of 10W-30 and spraycans of lock de-icer, a little radio is crackling away, caught between two AM stations. I ring the bell and wait. In the back I hear the sound of a throat being cleared. Fisher appears, with a preprogrammed smile on his face. He's doing up his belt buckle. He walks around the counter.

'Hey, boss!'

These will be his last words with an intact maxillary lateral incisor. A single right hook, a transfer of weight, a precisely calibrated impact. With his hand on his jaw, Fisher shakes a bit, grimaces, and spits out a chunk of tooth.

'Fair enough,' he says. Then he's smiling again.

I now have three reddish-pink fingers and a spring in my step. I go back to meet Marie out on the sidewalk. She nods, aware there's nothing she can say. To speak she'd have to use those selfsame lips that last night failed to push him away, in the depths of our boredom. For the first time since we got here, I think I'm happy.

'Well, should we get started? On this new life of ours?'

'I guess we should.'

I take Marie's hand. She doesn't demur. We move forward slowly, admiring the banality of our surroundings. The trees. The road. Plants and houses, insects and concrete, dust suspended in the air. Burgeoning forest, mouldy particle-board over windows. Peeling paint. The village supine on a bed of dead leaves, waiting to die as the greenery gnaws at its extremities.

Every day an old person leaves town or passes on. Someone who was determined to stay to the bitter end throws in the towel and promises never to return, not even to watch the bulldozers eviscerate their childhood home. Forty years from now, this playground Marie and I stopped by will be long gone, like the rest of this place. Nature will reclaim its own, any foxes that remain around here will have free rein of the territory, with no notion that, once upon a time, here stood a rusty merry-go-round on a cement pad with a heart carved into it.

Marie sighs. I can tell she's thinking about the Lavoie children, imagining them whipping down the slide that stands there on rusted posts, climbing the spiderweb, and spinning around the merry-go-round. She knows they most likely never come here. The sand is smooth. From where we stand, we can see the antenna, off in the distance, in the forest. Not one single bird sings.

With a stern look, Marie stares at the swings. I can tell she doesn't share my happiness, but I have no idea how to cheer her up.

'Think we'll need a Ski-Doo?'

'Why?'

'I don't know. I just have a feeling we're going to need a Ski-Doo here.'

'We're also going to need a hot water tank. But I'm not sure the guy who can put a new one in will feel like doing it.'

'I can handle it.'

'No, you can't.'

'Yes, I can. You'll see.'

We keep strolling. I haven't managed to make her crack a smile, but at least we're walking. I think about all the work to be done back at the house: the bathroom drywall, the half cord of wet wood we'll have to cover. Marie turns around and takes a final look back at the park.

'I love you,' I say.

She nods, as if I'd asked her a question. Little by little my eyelids are drooping, my good spirits wearing thin. We keep walking.

Just in front of us, a root has proven stronger than the sidewalk concrete. We don't see it, though, and both trip at the same time. It's out of sync, like a poorly executed dance move with no music. Marie regains her balance, but no such luck for me: I hit the pavement knee-first and tear a hole in my pants. Marie laughs and I think I see the sunlight in her right eye, the one that squints just a touch more than the left. God, she's beautiful when she laughs. I should fall more often.

I get up, dust off my clothes, and pretend to be angry. She keeps right on laughing, to hold on to it until another person breaks in on us, but the moment she sets eyes on the park behind us, the red and the yellow and the sand and the absence of footprints, Marie's smile is gone. The fragile light in her eyes goes out, and she moves forward into the emptiness. I follow her. I know that the moment we get home she'll take two or three pills in front of the bathroom mirror. It'll be her turn to fall.

~

The late-May sunshine slips through the slats in the blinds the old guy must have put up a thousand years earlier. Marie's skin is creased, yet soft and smooth, and for once she lets me look at her body. We have sex again because it's what we have to do, but today there's a little extra heart and vigour in it, bundling us in a layer of warmth, pleasure, or maybe happiness, perhaps even cautious optimism.

'That was good.'

'…'

'I love you.'

'…'

'For real.'

Marie pulls the blankets up to her neck and closes her eyes.

'I'm not going to say it, Marie.'

'But you're thinking it.'

'No. Yes. I don't know. It seems like we'll have to start believing. That's why we came here, right?'

A year and a half earlier, when we'd only been trying for a few months and we could still talk and even laugh about it, Marie's obnoxious co-worker Daphne was always there with inane advice for us. *Don't worry, six months is nothing. It's totally normal, don't worry.*

Everything's going to work out fine. So, for at least a month we did our best to laugh about it. It was normal, after all. Everything was going to be fine. But of course nothing was really going to be fine. Everything was going to go sideways. We may not have known for sure yet, but we both had a pretty good feeling.

In what was probably an attempt to convince myself, I repeated the same words like a mantra after every time we had sex: *this will be the time.* Marie stopped believing first. I followed suit not long after. I said it a few more times anyway, like a prayer – I was sure of it – but my phony enthusiasm was repellent even to me, so I stopped.

'You're right. That's why we came here. But what if it doesn't work? What will we do if I can't get pregnant? How long do we stay if …?'

'Let's start by getting settled in … It's already getting to be more fun, right? At least there's that. Maybe we can find each other again. This'll help us.'

'I guess so, yeah.'

'Marie … I really want us to make it work here.'

'Yeah. Me too.'

'Everything's going to be be okay.'

'Don't say that.'

It may just be me, but I'm starting to believe in all of it: our house, this two-bit town, our exile. We'll fill that park with little ones. We have to.

❧

I put my hand on Marie's stomach. She takes it and places it on her right breast. She has noticed my swollen knuckles and the impression Fisher's incisors have left in my flesh. She chooses not to mention it. It isn't the first time in my life I've hit someone. Yet I'm not a violent person.

I remember the weather station at the end of the street I grew up on. At least, that's what we thought it was. *We* was Lannie and I. The weather station was full of metal instruments, and we would make up names for them: ventilometer, thermo-dynamography reader, snow sieve, and of course the antenna of youth – that one was there solely to make the station look cool, as far as we were concerned. The whole set-up was protected by a fence taller than we were, with barbed wire, angled up at the top. If it weren't for that barrier of metal wire, we would have broken in and run around whenever we wanted. We were convinced that barbed wire, of the kind used to contain prisoners in our stories, could only be there to protect some fantastic treasure. We felt responsible, as if the entire set-up were some-how part of us.

I also remember a Grade 5 kid with a crooked tooth and a high voice. Eddie was a slowpoke with long fingernails and an evil stare. We steered clear of him as best we could. There were unsettling rumours about him, and we were pretty weak. One morning Lannie had a cold, and he stayed home hugging his mom's hot water bottle instead of dragging his feet through the wet snow with me. I saw Eddie from a distance, crouching in front of the weather station. He was gathering stones, filling up his pockets. He got up and started throwing them over the fence, at the equipment. Our equipment.

Without a second thought, driven by a visceral pain inside, I ran right up and yelled at him. *Stop, it's fragile!* The water in the corner of my eye wasn't melted snow. Eddie just laughed, the way his kind always do when they see that you care about some-thing, and kept right on throwing rocks. I backed up and took a swing, punched him right in the jaw, as hard as I could. His knees buckled. I didn't stay to watch the scene unfold, just turned around and ran toward school. I was terrified by what I had done but proud that I'd defended our treasure.

I never found out if I hurt him or not. But the days that followed were marked by that special blend of pride and fear experienced only by those brave souls who've had the courage to do something truly bad. Not long after, before he could exact his promised revenge, Eddie got kicked out of school. We never found out why. Conflicting stories made the rounds: Eddie had sworn at a teacher, committed an act of vandalism, master-minded a string of murders.

That Tuesday morning when I was nine years old was the first time I ever hit another person. My only prior victims had been the living-room couch cushions and the kitchen wall one time when my mom came home from the mall empty-handed. Later I'd put my fist to the test against more than one face, always right before the tears rose up and fogged my vision. I wish I had it in me to keep my cool when someone messes with something I hold dear, but Fisher's mouth reminded me that I probably never will. I'm not a violent person, though.

'Have I ever told you about Eddie?'

Marie has fallen asleep, with my hand on her breast and my swollen knuckles throbbing in time to her heartbeat. The memory of Eddie. My childhood. The weather station. The antenna of youth.

Simon's hand rests on my breast. He thinks I'm sleeping. It's not that his stories bore me, more like he's trying too hard to fill up the silences, patching the cracks in my life with little snatches of his own. It's exhausting. He means well. He wants to help me get better. I've heard him say exactly that: *I want to help you get better.* For a long time I let him be my crutch and let myself be his. But at times like these, and increasingly often, it's just too much, and I feel the need to fall on my own. So I pretend to sleep.

Simon withdraws his hand, tenderly brushing me with his fingertips. He slides off the mattress like the loveliest of snails. The floor creaks, then silence. I'm all alone, master of nothing, on an old queen-sized mattress in a room that smells like old people, humidity, smoke, and earth. It smells like my grandmother's.

She's the one who came with me to have an abortion when I was seventeen. She organized everything. I was catatonic, too young to handle it; she held my hand. I've never told Simon about it. On that day I felt like I should have been sad, or emotional, shaken up, but all I felt was embarrassed about bothering my grandmother. It took fifteen years for me to feel something, and then it wasn't the pain of having abandoned a piece of my own flesh but regret at giving up the very thing I now wanted. An alternate version, too old by now and scarred by a difficult childhood, but alive. If I'd kept her, I'd be a mother now, not just some woman who's been trying too hard for far too long with a partner who's too nice in a town that's too far away.

Against the wall, in the box marked 'Marie personal' in my own handwriting, all my secrets lie boxed up. The memories from each of the seasons of my gradual disillusionment. Letters suffused with the innocence of springtime, desiccated maple leaves pressed between the pages of notebooks, the lingering wafts of long-evaporated perfume, the ashes of our first winter loves.

A yellowed envelope at the very bottom of the box holds a letter given to me one January night by René, father of the fetus. He said he loved me and he always would. The bracelet he gave me was a token of this *always*. On his single bed, after making love, I told him I was pregnant, and he left me. Twenty-four hours later he vanished somewhere between Lacordaire Boulevard and Tanzania. If he'd stayed, I wouldn't have gotten an abortion.

In the backyard, Simon's pretending to sleep now. His chaise longue is buried under the long grass we'll have to mow sooner or later, maybe tomorrow. I'm going for a walk. It's mild out, the world is moving slowly, my footsteps applaud my numb forward motion.

In a town this small, there's no chance of getting lost.

There are clouds and quiet homes, and there's wind and a church. In a corner of the churchyard, thousands of ants have gathered around a chunk of apple. Anne-Benedict is there, in sweatpants. I try to avert my eyes. She's not running; she's speed-walking. It's the easiest thing in the world for her to stop next to me. I'd rather she fast-jogged right by and drove her Spirit of America roadster into the horizon with no parachute. But no.

'Marie! Are you looking for something? You seem lost.'

'Hi, Anne-Benedict – '

'Anne. Just call me Anne.'

'Okay. No, I'm fine. I'm just out for a walk. Simon is sleeping.'

'You should walk with me! We'll have *a ball*! And it'll keep us in shape.'

'Yeah, but I don't know … Is your husband looking after the kids?'

'Yeah, they're crafting in the yard. Making a little something special just for me!'

I nod. They're the perfect family, hence insufferable. Simon will like them better than I do, I'm sure. He has a gift for looking like he's not paying attention to people yet conveying that he likes them. I'm the opposite: only by smothering them in compliments and peals of laughter can I manage not to terrify them.

'That's fantastic! Your kids are so cute. I can't wait to get to know them better.'

'Want to come over later? You could see their craft project!'

This prospect makes me vaguely nauseated, but I hide it. No, I don't want to drop by later. I already have too much to lose to agree to further humiliation in other people's backyards. What I want is to traipse around town without a clue where I'm headed.

'That's nice of you, Anne, but … another time, for sure. I have to go to the garage right now.'

'Car troubles?'

'Water heater.'

'Fisher can fix that for you.'

'So I heard.'

She touches my shoulder and leaves behind a film of sweat that reminds me of one of those interminable work nights. Forced smiles, friendships rotten on the inside. We'll be happy here, despite the Lavoies.

Anne-Benedict waves – *We'll do it again sometime!* – and then she strides off toward her goal: a level of physical fitness that will fill her with plenitude and joie de vivre. I set off in the opposite direction. The last few years have ground the spring from my step. It's the exact opposite of physical fitness. Despite everything, I don't envy Anne-. Just Anne.

I had no idea where I was going, and it was perfect that way, but now I have no choice. People say everyone knows everything about everyone in small towns; if I don't go right now and have a nice chat with Fisher about hot-water-tank oxidation, word will get around quickly. It's not like I'm exactly keen to meet him again. The impression of his lips on mine is still fresh. But I don't want to get a reputation as a liar. Especially on my first day here.

I come up to the service station. The butterflies in my stomach are fluttering in time to the rustling of the bushes that mark a line between the business and an abandoned house next door. I shouldn't be nervous, but the idea that Fisher might want to kiss me again disturbs me.

I walk past the bushes as a Chrysler rolls up. It seems larger than this whole town. Fisher stares at me impassively, then susses out the car. His mind made up, he signals, with one hand, to wait, while caressing the car's side panel with the other. He stares at the gas cap. The grease-smeared fingerprints. Mechanical affection. And me, waiting for something whose nature I don't know the first thing about. I hold the bracelet René gave me like a rosary, telling the multicoloured beads, though my prayer is monochromatic, *Good God, please tell me what I'm doing here.*

The large American lady leaves an olfactory memory of an overfilled tank and burnt oil, and Fisher wipes his hands on his thighs as he comes over toward me.

'Hi.'

'Hi, Fisher.'

'What are you doing walking? Ran out of gas? I've got some old gas cans, if you need – '

'No, I was out for a walk.'

'Walking?'

'It's not a big town.'

'Yeah, but driving is faster.'

'I'm not in a rush.'

I look into his eyes, searching for any sign of emotion: desire or exasperation, sadness or disdain. I see nothing at all. He seems to barely recognize me. Sheer indifference. I look down.

'Did you come here to see me, or –'

'Yeah. Actually, I don't really remember, but yeah, I came here. I … I have something for you.'

I hand over René's bracelet. He takes it.

'What's this?'

'A bracelet. It has a sentimental value for me, but I wanted to give it to you. An apology for my boyfriend. For your tooth.'

'It was already broken.'

'Still.'

'Okay, thanks.'

He turns around and walks away. I call out to him.

'Do you remember kissing me yesterday?'

'Yeah. Thanks for that too, I guess.'

And he's off. I don't know what I came here for, but what I've found has undermined me – as if I had been hoping he'd jump my bones, and now his indifference has hurt me. I'm not that girl. I think what I was hoping for was the chance to turn him down. Do what I should have done yesterday, make it right, turn my head and walk away, give him a kick.

He comes back.

'You know, sweetie … I don't remember your name. Did I ever get your name? Anyway, sweetie, you know … People are kind of like the shocks on old cars. You can bend 'em up and all around a thousand times, and they'll absorb it for a long time, but sooner or later they're gonna snap. And when they snap, there's no fixing 'em.'

'I –'

'Don't do your snapping here, okay? We've got enough on our plates with our own shit.'

Fisher disappears behind a wall of old tires before I get the chance to answer. I wouldn't have known what to say anyway.

⁓

We'll soon see how small towns are more stifling than big cities. We came here in search of a particular peace that we felt we deserved: wide-open spaces and tall grass and silence and no one around. We escaped the crowds to bury our paltry sorrows and tend to our grand hopes, in the peace and quiet of the countryside. But we forgot one fundamental truth: bombs sound loudest in the desert.

I am getting ready to leave, fully prepared to run or even speed-walk, anything to put miles between myself and the service station, when Madeleine accosts me from across the street.

'Hey!'

She beckons me to cross over to her side. I'm not really in the mood, but her tone of voice leaves no room for a noncommittal wave and swift escape.

'Hey!' I reply.

I cross the street. She's not smiling. She speaks slowly.

'You know, I really want to like you, honey. I'm happy to serve you eggs in the morning and I won't charge you much.

But you gotta realize that we don't really like new people around here. It's not your fault. You guys seem nice and all. But sometimes you just gotta know when to stay in your lane.'

This from Madeleine who'd been so friendly just this morning. Confusion must be written all over my face.

'Just try to understand me, honey. People like you, who aren't from here. You guys and the Lavoies too. We're happy to have you at the restaurant. It's business, and we like the conversation. Lord knows we don't have much of either these days.'

'Yeah. We had a good time this morning.'

'The thing is, though, when I see you here talking to Fisher, giving him a little something. I don't want to know what – '

'It was nothing. Just – '

'I told you I don't want to know. Fisher doesn't need that. And yesterday, he didn't need you to go pulling your little dress up over your thighs at the bar.'

'What? But I didn't – '

'Linda told me everything. You know us waitresses talk. I don't know what you're playing at, girlie, but I don't need that. Things are hard enough already. We're struggling here. You know, when a town is slowly dying, a lot of old wounds come to the surface. And ever since they put in the antenna – '

'That antenna again? What's up with that antenna?'

'If I were you, I'd stick close with the Lavoies. Enjoy the peace and quiet. And leave us locals alone.'

I don't answer.

'But if you want breakfast, come by the restaurant any time.'

She smiles, then pops back into the restaurant, leaving me shell-shocked on the sidewalk. From across the street, Fisher watches me. Expressionless. Worrying René's bracelet.

There's half a cord of wood stacked against the side of the house. Simon is limply patting the log pile. The wind kicks up. So does my guilt. I haven't lied in a long time, but I know it's the right course of action. He'll ask me about my walk, and I'll leave out Fisher and the bracelet. I'll give him Madeleine, maybe Anne's kids crafting her some marvellous present in a backyard where the grass is green, thick, and freshly cut. It could be that Madeleine's right, we should keep to ourselves. If our aim is to build a third human being inside me, it'd be better to start off with just the two of us, far away from everyone else and their fears, far from the burnt eggs and motor oil. We can focus on our little lives in the bottom of our little crater. I'll lie.

Simon points at the wood. I'm not really interested.

'It's way too wet … '

'No big deal.'

'I just really wanted to make a fire tonight … '

'I love you.'

Simon suddenly forgets all about our logs. We'll have all summer to make fires. The country evenings are cool. He takes my hand with a concerned look.

'You okay?'

'The waitress this morning … I think she … threatened me.'

'You went back to the restaurant?'

'I went for a walk. She came over and talked to me.'

'What'd she say?'

I paint him a picture, one that doesn't include Fisher. He nods. I know he finds all of this funny but is afraid to show it. All this unknown drama is a diversion to him, and that's part of why he agreed to follow me here. To see our problems dissolved in with other people's. It's a new recipe we're trying out.

'Don't worry about her. She's just looking for attention.'

'She mentioned the antenna too.'

'Was Fisher there?'

'No.'

There. I lied.

❧

A blue shadow seeps into Marie's eyes when she lies. There's also a nervous twitch at the base of her neck. It doesn't happen often, and it doesn't bother me. But we've only been here a day, and we've been lying from the moment we got here. Every time we say, 'Life is going to be good here,' and 'We need to celebrate.' One more lie can't hurt me. There will be others, and I'll lie about them too. Little splashes of falsehood we'll sop up with all our 'I love yous,' because the 'I love yous' are true and always will be.

Marie is tracing semicircles with her foot on the packed dirt next to the car, as the wind slowly undoes her work. She's run out of things to say to cheer us up. Since we got here, every silence amplifies the fear hanging over our heads, the fear that we've made a terrible mistake.

'I'm going to go see the antenna,' I tell her. 'I'm intrigued.'

'I'll make pasta. Come back quick, okay?'

I promise. Marie retreats to the house while I try to figure out the best route to my destination. Three hundred feet away, by the bar full of tight-lipped drinkers, I can see the antenna about half a mile in front of me, up where the clouds are waiting for me and the first raindrops will greet me, a swath cut into the wall of branches in the forest. The path is narrow, but the traces of other footsteps in the dirt make it clear I'm not lost. The rain falls on me, undeterred by the trees' sparse leaves. I feel the wind swirling around my ankles and breathe in the petrichor. The sun disappears.

I slip between the tree trunks and follow the zigzag traced in the muck by the people who've come before me. I've been walking a long time, though the antenna appeared so close to the road. I slip and grab on to a tree trunk for support. The bark is frozen. I shiver – from my fear or the cold, I'd rather not know. The rain kicks up, as always, and every raindrop feels like the past tapping me on the shoulder to remind me that I'm not alone and never will be.

It's dark now. I still can't make out the antenna, but I can feel a vibration, like a faraway moan or gasp of pain. Then I see it: a commanding presence in the middle of nowhere. I shouldn't be impressed, but I am. It's no more than an object, a metal structure. Even if I know, deep down, that it's probably just Fisher's and Madeleine's stories messing with my mind, I also sense that there's more to it. I'm sure of it. Protected by a massive fence, it somehow crushes and compresses me. I feel tiny at its foot. The dirt all around the tower has been tamped down and worn away by the footsteps of visitors who must have gathered around it, and for all I know still do. But why?

I can sense that I should turn around, walk away, and never come back; I should tell Marie I couldn't find it, lie or no lie. I can feel that the thing I'm about to discover will bring us no reprieve. But the rain under my shirt, dripping down my spine, pushes me forward. It's getting harder and harder to breathe.

Oxygen is swirling around the antenna with every minuscule vibration of the metal; it feels like I'm drowning. I get down on one knee.

Farther ahead I see a break in the fence enclosing the antenna. Its links have been twisted and pulled up at least a foot off the ground in one spot. I get down on all fours and crawl through the muck, under the fence, spurred on by the need to breathe, the desire to press up against the steel and reclaim all the air the antenna has sucked from my mouth. I keep telling myself it's just a piece of metal, just a *thing*. As I run out of breath, I place my hand on the steel structure. A harsh draft fills my lungs and thousands of images flare up inside me, things I can feel but can't see. I relive the last three years, moment by moment, with such clarity that it feels just like real life. It's not a succession of memories, or the movie of my life, more like the truth that has always lain within me blowing up like fireworks on my skin. The truth I've been trying to forget because it hurts.

The clouds are black. The water is boiling, it burns me, my fingers are numb. I let go of the antenna and everything goes back to normal. It's just a thing, made of metal. I breathe in and out. I'm no longer drowning. The forest all around me hasn't seen a thing. Nothing happened here.

My pants are covered in mud.

I'll make up a story for Marie, tell her I was playing at doing basic training, or I got sucked into quicksand, or I read an article about how a mud mask would do wonders for my pores. I'll make her laugh, and she'll know I'm lying, but it'll be better than telling her the truth about what just happened. Which is nothing. Which has to be nothing. I'll tell her I didn't discover anything at all. Which will be a lie. I've learned that there's no point trying to forget.

I get up. Before I leave, I may as well walk around all four steel posts. That's when I see her. She must have been here from the start, but she hasn't said a word. Hasn't moved, not so much as a shudder. She's sitting in a quiet corner, leaning against the antenna, with a pen in her hand and her head down over the wet pages of a blue notebook. I jump a little when I see, but she doesn't react. A minute goes by. I watch the raindrops falling on her blond, almost white, short hair. She's soaked.

'Hi?'

No reaction.

'Hello?'

She raises her head and looks at me, calm as a beach in summer. She must be twenty, or not even. She looks me up and down, then throws me a bit of a smile. In those big black eyes I'll remember as long as I live, thousands of words are held captive, along with a certain sadness. Her ponderous calm eases my mind, and I almost stop thinking about the recent sensation of drowning and the little crusts of mud caked in the weave of my pants. Deep in her eyes I can see barbed wires, like the ones in my childhood prison stories, like the ones at the weather station. The kind that can only be there to protect a treasure.

Her name, I'll later learn, is Alice. She's beautiful.

'What are you doing here?' I ask.

She dives back into her notebook and turns a page. She keeps on reading.

'Are you … from here? Where do you live?'

She doesn't answer, or look at me, as if I'd disappeared, as if I'd only imagined that she'd turned to face me, or as if she were a figment of my imagination and had never seen me at all. Yet I feel the need to talk to her.

'I'm Simon. What's your name? Okay, don't worry about your name. I'm Simon. I just moved here, into the house … I think people call it the old guy's house. Is that … is that your antenna? I keep hearing about it. I wanted to know what it was, and I didn't want to bother you. I wanted … I shouldn't have touched it. Does it do that to you too? It doesn't really seem like it. Doesn't it hurt you? Maybe I'm just not used to it. What are you writing in your notebook? None of my business, I know … '

The more she ignores me, the more I want to talk to her. If I'd run into her in the city, say in the throng of people on the sidewalk on Sainte-Catherine Street, I wouldn't have given her a second glance. But we're all alone here. Just me and those big black eyes.

'What does this antenna do? How did they install it here? What's your name? We came here because nothing was working for us anymore in the city. The crowds were killing us. Know what I mean? We needed room to breathe, to be out in nature. Forests, rivers. And to be around normal people too. Where we were living, there wasn't a single normal person left in our social circle. We pushed away everyone who was still willing to put up with us. We ran away, I guess, and ended up here. We ran away. Doesn't the rain bother you? How'd you get in here without getting dirty? I had to drag myself through the mud. I'm filthy. No big deal, the rain is warm. The clouds are low, hey? I like clouds.'

She closes her eyes. I take two steps back.

She curls up with her knees against her chest and her notebook pressed tight against her body. She doesn't move. I don't move either.

'I like clouds,' I say again.

The next two minutes that go by feel like months, like summer storms raging while fall winds blow leaves from the trees before they've even finished growing, all at once. I slide under the fence again. Once I reach the narrow path, I take another look back at Alice. She hasn't moved an inch.

As I make my way back home, I replay every second of our encounter. I don't know why, but I'm afraid of forgetting. Yet that's exactly what I have to do: forget. The clouds drift off.

I get undressed on the doorstep, as Marie watches and laughs at me.

'Did you win?'

'What?'

'Your mud-wrestling match. Did you at least win?'

'I had to crawl. To get under a fence.'

'And? Was it worth it? What's so special about that antenna?'

'Nothing. Just a standard broadcast antenna. Large. Four metal support beams.'

'It's an antenna.'

'Yup.'

'And that's all you found out there?'

'Yup.'

We tell ourselves lies in order to survive. Trade them, like kids with their old toys. In this town that's a foreign land to us, we'll learn to invent those truths that provide the greatest succour. I now know we'll never be able to forget the past, but that's exactly what we're trying to do, despite it all. Forget the past, love each other in the present moment. Cut off from the world, we'll conceal our scars beneath the sleeves of our false hopes.

When we die a few months from now, it will be the most beautiful day of our lives. Until then we'll survive, just as long as our secrets remain intact.

~

I'd been hoping for roosters. It's not like I enjoy getting up early, but if we're going to embrace country living, we may as well go whole hog. The thing is there aren't any roosters around here. No birds at all, which Marie finds disconcerting. A few times now we've left the window of our little backroom open all night, and today around five in the morning, with her eyes wide open and goosebumps on her arms, she heard a faraway noise of a car door slamming shut. Then the silence set in and stayed right through the fall. If there are birds here, they aren't singing.

'It's not normal.'

I sleep in a little. Just a little longer, okay, just a few more minutes. I'm half-asleep, in a cocoon of sunshine and warmth, and I don't really feel like dealing with Marie's qualms.

'It's just not normal, Simon. I'm telling you. Even in the city you can hear the birds singing at five in the morning. Here there's not even a peep.'

'Want me to sing for you?'

She gets out of bed, with scrunched-up eyebrows and a cheerfulness wholly unnatural this early in the morning. I'll join her a few hours later, woken by loud knocking on the door coupled with inhuman squealing.

Downstairs, the Lavoie kids are climbing on the moving boxes we haven't gotten around to unpacking, which is to say all of them. I hurriedly get dressed and go down the stairs that bear the scuffmarks of the old guy's shoes. It's nice out, but too hot in the house. Patrick Lavoie, the little genius who can 'count up to ninety-three, can you believe it?' has opened up our boxes of winter coats, while his younger sister Delphine is trying one on. The peals of laughter from under the goose down and the screeches of delight in the Gore-Tex are so loud I can't hear what Anne-Benedict is saying to Marie. No great loss, since I couldn't care less. I take a moment to watch the children, until I hear a sound. Patrick is tearing the left sleeve of my pale blue jacket.

'Hey! Cut it out!'

Young Delphine freezes. Her eyes fill with tears before I can even shut my mouth. I already feel guilty: clearly, she's a precocious manipulator. Patrick prefers to ignore me and keep on digging through the box marked 'Winter,' like an intrepid archaeologist. He finds a pair of leather boots and thrusts an arm into each one. I give up. I didn't come here to raise other people's kids. In the kitchen, Marie is making coffee in a paroxysm of vernal joy.

'Look who *popped by* for a visit!'

Anne-Benedict responds with a round of applause, obliterating every lingering doubt that any attempt to like her will be futile.

'Hi, Simon! Just yesterday your wife was telling me how you guys wanted kids. So I thought I'd bring mine over for you to play with!'

'Really? She never told me that.'

'They made me a clay ashtray yesterday!'

'She didn't mention that either.'

'She couldn't have known. *I* didn't even know: they surprised me!'

If only I had even the slightest desire to understand any of this. I catch Marie having a private laugh off in her corner and see a reflection of the morning light in her right eye, the one that squints more than the other. I notice how beautiful she is.

'The water in the pool probably hasn't warmed up yet. But don't forget: you guys have an *open invitation!*'

'How could we forget?'

I'll keep making conversation for what will feel like entire days, under the affectionate eye of Marie, who will contribute almost nothing. From time to time she'll glance into the hallway to check on Delphine, who'll be wearing one of Marie's hats, or a pair of overalls, or the longest yellow scarf in the western hemisphere. Each time she'll feel like smiling but will hold herself back. Each time I'll find it harder to untie the knots in my entrails.

Patrick yells loudly and continuously, and frequently makes his sister cry. 'Settle down, little angels!' says Anne-Benedict from a distance, unconcerned by these words' total lack of effect. The kids are drinking orange juice. 'Do you have any? You know *how important* it is to get enough vitamin C!' We'll keep drinking coffee until Anne-Benedict can't take any more, since 'over three cups and I go *totally cra-zee!*'

Our morning will unfold like the hours before childbirth: painful and seemingly interminable. When the lulls in the conversation grow too heavy – over thirty seconds, at less than five-minute intervals – Anne-Benedict and the kids will leave to go swim in their not-yet-warm pool, and I'll dream of doing my own round of applause, but I'll refrain.

A few minutes later, when Marie and I are celebrating finally being alone again, we'll hear a quiet knock on the door. It's Delphine, returning a purple mitten of Marie's she'd hidden in the bottom of her gumboot. I thank her and raise my head toward the sidewalk to give Anne-Benedict my sweetest smile – but I freeze. In the background, a few steps behind the Lavoie family, Alice is standing on the sidewalk, with her blond hair and black eyes, observing the house, avoiding making eye contact with me. When the Lavoies are gone, she beckons me over.

With no clear sense of purpose or shoes on my feet, I walk toward her. Every painful step makes me wince as the gravel digs into the soles of my feet. Still she avoids my gaze. I can't get her attention. I'd like to ask what she's doing here, but I fear a repeat of yesterday, minus the rain. We're in public to boot, with Marie watching through the window.

Alice silently hops from foot to foot awhile. I don't know what she's waiting for. I don't know where to stand, or what to do. Finally, with trembling hand, she passes me an envelope. I take it. She hurries off without saying goodbye. If she were five years younger, she'd probably be running, but in her twenties she's developed a modicum of restraint.

In the envelope is a half-sheet of paper. The ink has run; the handwriting looks rushed.

*My name is Alice. I'm deaf and mute. Sorry about yesterday: I
didn't mean to insult you by not talking to you. Again, I'm sorry.
I won't bother you anymore. Please grant me the same courtesy.*

I look up. Alice is long gone.

'Who was that?' asks Marie, from the doorstep.

'A girl I ran into when I went to see the antenna yesterday. She seemed really weird, but now I get it. She's deaf.'

I think Marie has further questions. But I can also sense that she knows I have a few questions of my own. Sometimes the best solution is to remain silent. Like one of those wars that ends before the first casualty. That must be what the birds around here tell themselves.

We didn't come to the country to bother anyone, yet for the last twenty-four hours that's exactly what we've been doing. Madeleine, Fisher, Alice.

'We don't need them, do we?'

'Don't need them at all.'

Today's the beginning of our new life. We're going to fade into the woodwork. High time too. Marie and I, united against nothing in particular. We're here to make her belly swell until new life bursts forth. That's the one reason we're here, and we're going to survive.

⁓

Simon closes the front door and I grapple with the deadbolt. There's no need to discuss what we're doing. In this small town, like everywhere outside the city, everyone leaves their doors unlocked until the hardware gets jammed in position by the cold and rust and damp. World wars and earthquakes and countless deaths and births have come and gone in the century since someone used this lock. I yank, I push with all my might; I really don't think Ali Baba or Harry Houdini could do much better. I put my weight behind it, throw all my conviction into it – in vain. A drop of sweat rolls down my chin. I'm frustrated, but before it can fully catch flame, my anger is assuaged by Simon's ethereal laugh. He's laughing at me. It's the single tenderest thing he could possibly do. I also break into a laugh. I'm comfortable with Simon. It's in moments like these that we find our space again, our black sky teeming with the stars of yesteryear.

'Don't worry about the lock. Let them come into our house. We'll hide in the yard.'

Out in the yard, we're building an invisible anti-nuclear, anti-gravity shelter. Our reinforced-concrete cocoon contains a small arsenal. The wood we've set aside has begun to dry. Things we don't know how to do: dry wood, build a fire in the yard, find a path back to happiness.

We've been sitting in the grass in silence for hours, lulled by the wind. At one point I think I heard Delphine yelling in the distance, and we both spontaneously smiled, with no need to exchange a glance or plug our ears. Evening came. The long grass folded over like waves at high tide. Simon stacked a few logs into a hopeful pyramid, and I stuffed months-old newspapers into the remaining orifices, and we spent a long time looking for matches. It was my turn to laugh at Simon as he pretended to know how to make a fire; he laughed at me as he blew on it pointlessly. And together we laughed at Anne-Benedict.

'Oh my, I just can't wait take a dip in that pool!'

'Oh my god, me *too*! Think we'll get to see her ashtray?'

'You mean the *surprise* ashtray those *adorable* little kids made for their *perfect* parents?'

'Little mitten thieves!'

'That's *exactly* what happens when you take too much vitamin C.'

We're pretending to hate her much more than we actually do, just like we're pretending to find her kids insufferable to make our own solitude a little more bearable. They're the kids we don't have, and we hate Anne-Benedict and Christian for being the parents we aren't.

This morning, when Delphine leaped on me, I took a step backward. I was somehow disgusted, or hateful, or scared. The way I reacted embarrasses me. I don't think anyone noticed, but

I'm still thinking about it tonight. Clearly I'll be a bad mother. One of the ones who may look after her kids but never finds a way to love them unconditionally. It's not what I want, but it's the way it's going to be.

'It's going to work, right, Simon?'

'What do you mean, *it*?'

'I'm going to get pregnant.'

'Of course you will.'

He believes it. It's the same tone of voice as the first time he ever told me we'd be together forever. The tone of a truth solid enough to grasp on to and pull yourself out of the mire.

'You know, the other night. With Fisher. I didn't do anything. He's the one who … I didn't want to … '

'I know.'

'For real.'

'It's no big deal. We're here now. Just you and me. In our backyard. We've got this fire to ourselves.'

We have to dance. In this ebony silence, in this grass up to our calves, huddled around a tepid fire that refuses to catch. Between our still-frozen bodies and the prospect of Siberian sex, we need to dance. The coals of this reluctant fire aren't lighting up the yard enough for us to be embarrassed to be shaking our asses out in this silent night. Simon takes my hand. He's dragging me onto the dance floor. Our bodies awkward and shy, the soles of our feet soaked in dew. Twigs tickle our wounds, and before long an imaginary rhythm takes hold, and I see the shadow of a smile stealing over Simon's face. We need to dance and dance and dance some more. Start off with small awkward steps, as if we were partying at some cheap roadhouse in an industrial park. Then our movements fall into a pattern. We cha-cha-cha with brio, throw in a few merengue, salsa, and tango moves. I trample Simon's foot.

Simon pulls me tight to him. He calms me down just like he always does. It's his great gift.

'Already time for the slow dance?'

'Seems like it.'

'But can you hear it? It's a disco song.'

'I know.'

He slows the rhythm down a bit more and brushes my neck with his lips. He whispers.

'We're the real deal. You and me, kid. I mean, if we can pull off a disco slow dance?'

I kiss him. He kisses me. A few minutes later we'll be swinging our asses again to another imaginary song. We'll pretend it's Dalida.

No alarm wakes us the following morning. We've stopped turning it on, out of sheer laziness. We while away the lazy hours in a sun-drenched stupor. Simon gets up. It's noon. I thought I heard a cat outside. I've started eating peanut butter for lunch and washing my face with men's soap. We got here three weeks ago, and I still haven't explored our lot. It's something to do, I guess. Simon flops out. His back is arched, and he has a tender look in his eye. I go out. We seriously have to mow the lawn. And for that, we need a lawn mower.

At the little grocery store the old owner eyes me suspiciously. Up till now it's always been Simon who comes here to pick up fruit and a carton of eggs. And bacon.

'You're the wife. The other guy's wife.'

'Yeah.'

'I wasn't sure. I'm not so good at remembering people. You look a little like Mrs. Lavoie.'

'Oh, no … '

First he insults me, then he follows me around his grocery store. The days must be long behind the counter of a deserted business. Before a mirage of potentially interesting conversation, the old man is bewitched. Clearly, he doesn't know me yet.

'So you live in the old guy's house.'

'Yup.'

'It's a nice place.'

'Yup.'

'You don't talk much, hey, lady?'

'Nope.'

'The old guy was like that too.'

'You don't say.'

'That's right. Didn't talk. Didn't smile much either. Kind of ugly too, if you ask me. Not that I could tell you what makes a man good-looking. No sir, I like women. Pretty women. Like Madeleine. Do you know Madeleine? Now there's a beautiful woman. But the men around here are kind of ugly, if you ask me. Take Big Bert, who had the grocery store before me. He was … '

Now, I would much rather have filled my cart in silence than listen to this disquisition from the head jury member of the Mr. Middle of Nowhere Pageant. But it did get me thinking. A man lived in our house for decades, and we don't know the first thing about him. A man who knew every inch of our home by sight and by touch, from the foundation to the chimney flashing.

'Did you know him well?'

'Big Bert? Worst man to ever walk the earth.'

'No, the guy you call the old guy.'

'Oh, the old guy. Yeah, I knew him pretty well, I guess. A damn fool.'

'So you didn't like him?'

'No one liked him. Gotta say that he wasn't here all the time. He went to the city a lot. Other places too, all around the world, I heard. He was some kind of big shot. Or at least that's what he'd say. For me he was always just the old guy with the nice house.'

I'm missing a bag of onions, but I don't care. I also don't care about the shopping basket handles cutting off my circulation, or my plans for tonight's dinner. What's bothering me is the fact that the man who lived out his life within the four walls of our home was universally disliked. From the moment I set foot in his home, I took for granted that he was a good man. The place was redolent of warmth, and love, though it went to seed a bit in the last few years, after he died. Even Simon, when he pushed open the door, said he could feel the presence of a big heart.

'He couldn't have been that bad. Why didn't you like him anyway?'

'Hmm.'

The grocer looks down and uses his foot to sweep a dust bunny under the shelving unit. He swallows his saliva like a teenager who doesn't know what to say when his girlfriend starts crying. I press him.

'Why didn't you like him?'

'Actually, truth be told, I liked him okay when he was alive. Everyone liked him okay. We were proud of him. It's only after he died that we started to hate him. We all have our reasons.'

'What about you? What's your reason?'

'I grew up here. This here is my home, and I love my home-town. But things have been tough for a good while now. Since the factory closed down, that's when things started getting tough. And the old guy, well. It's like I told you, he was some kind of big shot. I don't know why. I never really understood what made him so special … '

'What did he do?'

'… but every time he went to the city, and every time he spoke on the radio, I kept hoping he'd talk about us. As long as he was alive, it was still possible. I spent years hoping he'd put this town on the map, and the factory would open up again. I was hoping he'd save this town. But no. He left not long after they put in the antenna. He never talked about us once. And the village kept dying, faster and faster. So I resented him. I still resent him. I hate him for not doing anything to help us before he left.'

'Maybe he couldn't?'

'But he was a real nice man – when he was alive, that is. He was a good person, the old guy. Always polite. Educated too. Like I said, a real nice man.'

'We'll try to live up to his example.'

'Do whatever you want.'

'I just meant that – '

'I won't be around that long anyway.'

'Why's that?'

'You didn't see the sign in the window? I'm closing the store in the fall. I'll move to the city, like everyone else. There's nothing left for me here.'

'But c'mon.'

'What's one more guy leaving?'

'Won't you miss it, though? Here, I mean.'

'Here? I've been missing this place for years.'

I wish I'd never given him the chance to open up. I should have just ticked off every item on my shopping list, paid in silence, and gone home without learning a single detail about the man who lived there before us, or the loss the whole town felt when he left. There was a time when I believed other people's sadness had the power to alleviate my own. But I take no joy in witnessing the defeat of an old man who loves his hometown. That'll teach me to open my mouth.

My fingertips are white and my shoulders hurt, so my basket must be full enough, even if I'm still missing something. I pay.

'Thank you. And I'm sorry, you know. About the town and all.'

He smiles for the first time, and I nod goodbye. I pull on the door at the exact moment someone else pushes from outside. I recognize that leather jacket: it's Fisher's. I look down and leave without looking at him. I go down the little staircase without a word and walk straight ahead without turning around. I see René's bracelet on his wrist. On my way back, I can't chase the grocer's story from my mind, but I'm pleased that I won't have to lie if Simon asks if I saw Fisher. Only a little white lie anyway.

❦

In the yard, Simon is stretched out on a chaise longue. I slide onto mine.

'I cut through the little park to go the grocery store,' I say.

'Bit of a detour.'

'There was no one there. I don't think the Lavoies go there.'

'Of course not. They've got their own freezing-cold pool!'

'Will we go to the park with our … with our kids?'

'Yeah, if we need to stop on the way to the grocery store.'

'It's a detour.'

'True.'

'Plus the grocery store is closing in the fall.'

'We'll just have to stop eating. It'll leave more time to play.'

The beer is warm and my hair is dirty, but Simon's presence and kind words are a balm this afternoon. We're idling away our days, one after another, and our chaise longues are turning into twin islands surrounded by a sea of yellowed lawn. We eat pasta with butter two nights out of three, and three quarters of our dishes still haven't been unpacked. We only go inside to have sex, and occasionally sleep, or to get our woollen blankets. We barely talk. It's just the ersatz peace we've been dreaming of. No bombs, no land mines; no flowers either.

This feels a lot like happiness, or something not far from it.

'Do you think it's empty?'

I wake up with a start. Simon apologizes: he didn't know, he thought that – it's no big deal, I'll fall back asleep later. He's pointing at the shed, with its peeling paint and sagging walls.

'Think it's empty?'

In our desperation to buy a house, any house at all, we didn't bother looking inside the shed on our sole visit. They told us this one had sat empty for three years, and from its crooked walls to its buckled floors, everything was just a touch askew. Why would the shed be any different? I'd already quit my job, and Simon had quit his, and we'd sold our house in the city. The thought of our savings eased our minds and we imagined ourselves lounging on chaise longues in the yard, watching our brood grow older as the years went by. We were passing through town when we saw the sign. It took just a few minutes peering into dirty windows, and it was a done deal. It had to be a done deal. It wasn't love at first sight, but it wasn't a rational decision either. More like an axe to the jugular. If we hadn't bought the house as is, without a second thought, then there would be a chance we'd change our minds and go back to the city, and going back to the city was the one thing we'd never survive.

'Must be empty, yeah.'

Simon gets up for the first time in eons. He ambles off toward the shed, and I follow. What are we doing, moving from our spot, walking, exploring – what if the shed is full of bombs and land mines?

The door is made of lumber and held closed only by a clutch of climbing vines. Simon gives it a good yank. My Hercules. Plants, grass, door, hinges: everything rips off in one piece. A humid warmth envelops us. Inside, the shed is much bigger than it looked from outside. The air is stifling, like a sauna. We'll be cooked in no time. Just next to the door there's a wheelbarrow full of rocks. A broken-tipped foundation screw leans against the wall. The two halves of an old beige toilet sit apart in the centre of the floor. And on the only shelf, near the back, there's a rifle and a metal box. A toolbox on the ground. Dust, rocks, and surely little bits of skin from the old guy who spent too much time hiding out in here. I hear a soft creaking.

Simon picks up the toolbox and puts it on the shelf, a transparent excuse to paw the rifle.

'Don't touch that.'

'Why?'

'It's not ours.'

'We bought it along with the house. I just want to take a look.'

'I said don't touch it.' I'm mad now. He's not backing down.

'C'mon, Marie. We don't even know whether it works. And I've always wanted to shoot a gun. I could learn to hunt.'

'Cut it out. You're not going to hunt, and you're not going to shoot a gun. Don't touch that shit.'

'I can do what I want.'

We'll go on saying nothing, loudly, just like every time we fight. We'll retrench our positions without arguments, repeat the same empty phrases with growing vehemence. Then we'll just stop. Simon will leave the gun on the shelf and promise never to touch it again. He'll also promise to repair the shed door, and then ask if he's allowed to touch the wheelbarrow. I won't laugh. I'll lie back on my chaise longue; he'll lie back on his.

The minutes go by, the wind and the clouds come back. A raindrop finds its way onto my neck. Simon sighs.

'This is such bullshit, Marie. Forty years from now, I'll tell the story of the one time in my life I almost got to touch a gun. And you'll say you don't remember, but I'll know it's not true. You'll totally remember.'

❧

It was fall. Simon and I had agreed to meet at the hardware store. At a time when getting outside and enjoying nature was all the rage, we spent our first date admiring common nails and two-by-fours. It was a bold move; I was charmed.

'The worst part is I'm not handy at all. I just thought it'd be funny.'

'It's true, it is funny. But I thought you'd be the kind of guy who can cut down a tree and build a cabin with the wood. I'm disappointed.'

'I could try right now. Where's the tree?'

We spent half an hour in the plumbing aisle. Simon chatted me up amid copper pipes and shower heads. I knew I'd kiss him before we even set foot in the caulking section. We held out another minute longer, just long enough to exchange a few lies, for the sheer fun of it.

'I'm a real woodsman. A log driver.'

'Yeah, I can tell, just by looking at you.'

'What do you do?'

'Trapper, mostly. I go out all winter, hunt bear pelts.'

'Explains the frostbite.'

'Yeah. I also deliver ice.'

'Who to?'

'People who need it, you know. And where do you your log-driving?'

'On the water. Most of the time.'

Then we cracked. He could see just far enough through the thicket of pleasantries to know the roots of us were already taking. That the natural force we'd spend nine years trying to outrun was already in the process of binding us together. We kissed under the neon lights, soothed by the sweet music of a key being cut on the grinder.

At the till, before we left, Simon stopped and turned toward me with a serious look on his face.

'Fifty years from now, we'll still be together.'

'Really?'

'Yeah. And we'll be happy.'

'Yeah. Fifty years from now.'

Simon never wavered from this prediction of where we'd find ourselves at seventy-five. Whenever we needed to remember that we loved each other, we'd repeat our little mantra, like a prayer, like a song. Fifty years from now. And since then we've often come back to it, especially when things are bad. To end a fight, to soothe a burn, to sand down the rough patches.

Forty-seven years from now, we won't remember, and everything will be okay.

Forty-four years from now, we'll tell our children about our first date at the hardware store.

Forty-two years from now, we'll be handsome and old and we'll still be laughing.

All that just to remember the roots that took on that fall day, almost ten years ago now. This summer we'll often have to return to this source of light to stanch our wounds with promises. *Forty years from now*, we'll say, over and over again.

❧

The deafening roar of the clouds. The sound of time standing still. The rustling of concrete pads. The swarms of ants colonizing town.

A yell. Half a second. Then more yells, lots of them, growing louder. A gut-wrenching sound audible from miles away. More violent than any storm, the wailing of a suffering child.

'I'm going to go see what's up. Call … I don't know. The police? An ambulance? It's coming from down there … From the antenna, I think.'

I run. Marie will follow a few minutes later. The screams are getting louder, ringing out through the streets of town and the rural road lined by abandoned houses. Fisher gets there at the same time as me, in his rusty pickup. We set off down the path, pushing branches aside as we go. The most tenacious of them scratch our arms. The antenna. Christian is shaking the fence with both hands and yelling things I can't understand, chewing on his words like a mad, salivating dog. He's slumped against the chain-link, mouth agape. Anne-Benedict holds Delphine in her arms. When the little girl tries to peer over the fence, her mother turns to shield her daughter's eyes, from what I still can't see.

'We were a little further off in the forest,' she explains. 'Picking wild raspberries. We didn't know he'd turned back. We always told him to stay away from the antenna. We had no idea he'd come back here.'

Fisher comes up to the fence. The screaming stopped a few seconds ago. I see it now: Patrick's little body, collapsed at the foot of the antenna, emptied out of all its screaming. His breathing is wheezy and halting. I shove Christian.

'What the hell are you doing?'

I drop to the ground and crawl under the fence, into the clearing I was in last time. I don't mind getting dirty for the son of these two deadweights. I wish I could understand their paralysis, but I can't. They're just standing there watching their son, who has fallen from a great height and hurt himself, not even trying to reach him. Fisher has gone back up the path to get help.

Marie arrives, panting, while I'm squatting next to Patrick. Her 'Oh my god!' is more convincing than the Lavoies' cries. Christian manages to wonder, 'What's he doing there?' Anne-Benedict, under Delphine's terrified gaze, just keeps repeating herself. 'We just went out to pick wild raspberries, we didn't know, we didn't know … '

'We don't care. Doesn't matter. We just have to help him. Now!'

The way I say it is harsh. It feels good.

Patrick fell from a good height, but he'll survive. He has to. A few broken bones, a head wound. His back isn't broken. It'll take a while for help to arrive. I stem the flow of blood from his most serious wound, check that he can tell me his name and age, and make sure he doesn't lose consciousness. I'd rather be here with him than talk to his parents, who have finally come up beside us next to the antenna.

Marie is short of breath. She's sitting up against a tree. A few minutes later, Fisher comes back with bandages and ice for the wounds, and bolt cutters for the fence. He goes at it, swearing, while I tend to the child's wounds as if I know what I am doing. When I look up, I see her off in the distance, hidden in the forest. Alice and those black eyes of hers with barbed wire deep within them, barbed wire reflecting the leaves and the tree. She's terrorized. I stare at her a long time. She doesn't react, but she sees me. Her mouth is open, her hands trembling. That might be a tear on her face. When night falls, we'll all have left the forest behind, but the antenna will remain.

As the ambulance finally drives off, Fisher, Marie, and I are left in the middle of the road, sighing as one. None of us had been prepared for such a brutal shock – us lounging on our chaise longues, Fisher getting oily knuckles under someone's Dodge. Patrick will be fine. We can all take solace in that, even if he's not the one in my thoughts. I can't get Alice out of my head. It's as if she were the one who suffered from the fall.

Fisher nods at Marie, then holds out his hand. I shake it. He gets into his pickup and drives off.

Marie wraps her arms around me. 'Should we go for a beer at the bar?'

'I'm all dirty.'

'I don't think anyone will mind.'

The bar is almost empty. Fisher still hasn't fixed the radio. We take a seat. Same table as last time, same chairs. Marie taps my thigh. She looks lovely tonight, even with dirt caked under her fingers and the terrified expression on her face.

'You may have saved his life, you know.'

'They wouldn't have sat around doing nothing until he died.'

'Well, it sure looked that way.'

'I wouldn't have had to save his life. He was fine. He was lucky. Little rascal.'

Red-haired, fair-skinned Linda comes over with two big Labatt 50s I didn't order.

'On the house. You saved the Lavoies' little brat.'

'How do you know about that?'

'There's no secrets around here.'

She goes back behind the bar. She's not smiling.

'Goddamn antenna, eh!' she says in a loud voice.

Two customers we've never seen anywhere else in town, customers who may well live at this bar, nod in agreement. Marie puts her finger on my forehead to wipe away some dirt.

'Why don't they like us?'

'Who?'

'The locals.'

'I don't know. We bother them.'

'But we'd stopped bothering them. Everything was going well. Why did the kid have to jump off the antenna like that? Why couldn't they just leave us alone?'

'I know.'

'I don't like this, Simon. We were fine, right?'

'Yeah.'

'I feel like everything is about to go wrong here.'

I wish I could tell her otherwise, but I can't. I feel the same thing she does, the tide turning against us. The feeling that the plutonic process unfolding in our depths these last few years is building to a finale; our crust is cracking, our fire dying out.

'Fucking antenna, eh?' yells Linda, one more time.

With its soundtrack of rumbling tires on asphalt, and the tinkling of rain on the roof, our car ride feels interminable. Marie wishes we'd gotten the passenger-side speaker fixed, but it's the destination more than the radio silence that's bothering her. The city. The hospital.

We go by our old house. A new mailbox, a fresh coat of stain on the door. Flowers, cosmos maybe. A dog.

When we get to the children's hospital, we find a parking spot right next to the main entrance. The kids must all be healthy today: no broken arms or stomach flus or bike accidents. Or maybe they're all dead. In the elevator a well-dressed sixty-year-old woman in a navy blazer with a white-and-gold brooch is holding a helium balloon. You have to find comfort wherever it's hiding, between the third and fourth floor next to the radiology department.

We were entertaining an impossible dream, hoping against hope that we'd find Patrick alone. That, in a great leap forward of maturity, he'd have asked his family to leave him alone to rest in peace. Then it would have been his parents' turn to go off and pick wild raspberries. But there they are at his bedside, except for Delphine. We soon learn that she's staying with her uncle Denis – we didn't ask his name, yet there it is. Anne-Benedict welcomes us with a flapping of arms, as if this were the best day of her life, and it's clear we'll have to hear all about her pool before we can talk about her son.

We learn from the duty nurse that Patrick has a cast but is in good spirits. He'll come away with no serious injuries. But I have to wonder whether falling from the antenna, in full sight of parents who were powerless to help him, will mentally scar him for life. Since we arrived, Anne-Benedict hasn't looked at her son, except to show us the Canada geese she drew on his cast. Christian is eating an apple, which he bites into and holds in his mouth to free up a hand to shake mine. He doesn't talk much, maybe because he's got an apple stuffed in his jaw, and when he looks at his son I can feel a parental tenderness I hadn't seen before in this family. It pains me, but I don't let it show.

I stay in my corner, leaning against the wall. As I watch them, I'm thinking something I could never admit to anyone: I wish Patrick hadn't survived the fall. I wish he was dead. That way Marie and I wouldn't be the only ones to know the exact feeling of that pain.

❧

She had just turned three. She was the most beautiful little fairy in the Milky Way, and to this day I cannot speak her name. She smiled even as she suffered, and she had Marie's mouth, and to this day I can't control my trembling at the image of those slightly crooked teeth she never wanted to brush. She died in this very hospital, three and a half years ago. She would have been six now. She'd be in school, and to this day I can't wake up in the morning without wondering what flavour of yogourt I'd put in her lunch if she were still with us.

Our daughter. Sickness and death. Here, far from there.

I've never found words to describe the deterioration right before we lost her. I can't explain what that particular suffering feels like. A pain like when your tooth is pulled out, but without end. They yank your molar out, and along with it comes every other aspect of your life, which was all somehow wrapped around the tooth. First your lungs are gone, you lose your breath. Burning throat, faltering heart; your bones, your blood. It's your blood that is dead, your muscles, your eyes your brain your tongue your nerves your nails, all of it ripped out from inside you, all attached to that one molar, all yanked out from your gums. It all happens so fast and yet it's all drawn out over such a long time that you are certain it will never end. There's always one more organ to rip out. There still remains an envelope of skin, and you are scrambling for your crutch, Marie, who's equally gutted and every bit as emptied out. You are the crutch of another crutch, like two communicating vessels: she fills you up with her tears while you fill her up with yours, all the cries held in before this tiny body you want to see move again, that you see moving, and you grab hold of your entrails and shove them back into the little hole in your guts but they won't fit in anymore, they pop back up and spurt out and you see the little body moving because if it doesn't move it means there's nothing else left, the past is all for naught, all human history and these countless wars have only led up to this, your minor tragedy. If her tiny body doesn't move, it means nothing exists, no gods, no stars above; it means you will never move again, and if you don't move again, it means you won't know what to do ever again, will never fathom how to live or why, and then you see it move again, that little lifeless body. Hear it quiver, feel the tickling on your fingertips the breath on your neck the laughter in the park on the swings and the hospital screams her lips on your skin, *Dad*, her hands clasping yours her fear of falling her fear of hurting herself her fear of leaving, in a hospital bed the fear of leaving and you fighting to keep your own fear hidden from her, your fear that grows exponentially by the second, fear of the void fear of insufficient oxygen fear of your crutch shattering to pieces, the end of everything, you'll always be a fraction of your former self, until death takes you, you'll ever and always be a mere fraction, never whole.

Our everything is pulverized in a crematorium, and the urn in the moving box reminds us we can no longer just be. Sure, we'll go on pretending. According to clock and calendar, we'll keep getting older. And we'll keep right on pretending.

Peace is a momentary void between two conflicts. My blood hurts; my blood will hurt forever. And every raindrop is her, our daughter come back to tap us on the shoulder; every drop of water is her, reminding us that we will never learn to endure this pain, compensate for her absence, rescind her departure.

⤚

Up till then, Simon and I had found ways to spend time with the Lavoies without thinking about *it* too much, despite this hospital and this city and our house, despite the succession of blows pummelling our insides from the moment we woke up that morning, despite our decision to make this visit, not so much for the sake of the Lavoies or their son, but more as a test for us, to see what we are made of, to see if we can hack it. We can't hack it.

Simon sighs, and I'm the only one who sees the massive tears behind the tight seal of his eyes. It was a common sight before she died, because we had to hide our anguish from her. Simon comes out of the room, and I immediately know where he's going; we met up in the intensive-care recovery room so many times that the floor must still be wet from our tears.

It's now my turn to sigh as I look at Patrick. I nod my head, and Anne-Benedict thinks my desperation must be directed at her. She touches my forearm and whispers to follow her to the room. She walks to the end of the hallway. There's a large window, a heater. I go with her. From here we can see the car in the parking lot. The rain. Anne-Benedict takes a deep breath.

'I know you and Simon don't like me.'

'That's not true. Not true at all.'

'I'm not stupid.'

'Listen, Anne. It's just not a good time.'

'It's just that no one in town will talk to us, so we were happy to meet you. But you don't have to … You're always welcome, but we're not forcing you.'

I don't know what to say, so I say nothing. Anne-Benedict looks at her watch. I go see Simon, with no idea whether I should be ashamed or satisfied after this conversation. I'll drive back to the town, and the noise of falling rain will drown out Simon's sobs.

Weeks have passed since our visit to the hospital, and Simon still hasn't gotten over it. Out in the yard, the July sun beats down on his forehead. He doesn't even notice. Our atonal daily existence is getting the better of him, a little more every day. He can no longer find it in himself to shoot me little smiles when he abruptly wakes me from my daily naps. He no longer goes out to the shed to finger the rifle in the hope of getting a rise out of me. I'd like to comfort him, get his mind off it, make him laugh.

I bought a lawn mower the day before yesterday. We still haven't touched it. My pain is swaddled and numbed; three years of fighting have left us hollowed out like bullet holes, chalky-dry as Gyprock, hard as rubble.

For four whole days I figured everything was going to be okay, and we'd be celebrating. I thought I was pregnant, imagined we'd achieved our objective, had taken up residence in a peaceful future and stifled the past. I'm not naive, I know the memory of our daughter will never fully leave us. She'll still be there with us years from now, alongside her little brother, and three years later when he outgrows her, she'll become the little sister. She'll still be there next to the little guy on the swing in the park, with messy hair and one unbuckled sandal. But she'll no longer be all alone, monopolizing every inch of our lives.

For four whole days I thought we'd cracked it, and a little saviour was making a home inside me. I didn't tell Simon, but he must have felt that something was different when I bought the lawn mower. I started moving. Squeezed oranges for juice. Then today my period came, and I just wanted everything to stop.

In our house the phone never rings.

A hydroplane flies over the town; we've seen it three times this afternoon. And every time, Simon and I look up at the sky, as if it might be something more than just a hydroplane.

'It hasn't rained for a long time,' Simon says.

'You're right. I'm not pregnant.'

'I know.'

'I thought I might be. But I'm not.'

'I know. I got it. You know how I can read your eyes.'

'You don't even look anymore … '

'I still look.'

He reaches a hand out to me. I take it. He caresses palm and thumb, and just then, at that precise moment, a little bit of life.

'Don't stop.'

He takes my hand and caresses my palm again for a few minutes, looking far away at the forest. He lets it go.

Don't stop. But this time I don't tell him, and I get up with no idea where I'm going. We're surrounded by an efflorescence, an almost stifling explosion of green. The shed door lying on the grass. Bits of dew concealed under blades of grass. An insect.

The spray insulation covering the shed walls **gleams** and sparkles. I cough. The dust that has gathered on the floor over years rises up to greet me in a cloud, even bigger than last time, as if you could cover up the whole town in it. I make my way forward. It feels like the shed is miles away. I'm thirsty, it's warm. Deserts of dust. Jungles. Dandelions on the wall. I've never touched a firearm.

❧

He walked up to us with a nervous look on his face and we knew right away the news was bad, but we never could have guessed just how bad. Slowly, he told us it was a rare disease and she was going to die and there was nothing we could do about it. He told us that she had six months to live. That they'd do everything they could to ease the pain, but it wouldn't be easy. That at the end she'd spend her last two or three months in the hospital. By that point we'd stopped listening. I was on the ground curled up into the smallest possible ball. I wanted her in my arms, in my body, right now; I wanted to scream into her ears it wasn't true, she wouldn't die, they were all wrong. Simon pushed the doctor as hard as he could. The doctor fell to the ground and apologized. At that exact moment, for us, it was somehow the doctor's fault.

This kind of thing didn't happen. Not to us. We'd always been lucky. There was just no way. She was coughing, she said it hurt, but surely it was nothing, surely this too would pass. It didn't pass. We had to go to the emergency room. They would make her better. They had to. But they didn't find anything wrong. They had to run more tests. They'd find it eventually, it would run its course, she would get better; that's how hospitals work. Children don't die, not here. Children live to be a hundred.

Nothing in the books you read can prepare you for this. Definitely not the brief chapter on coping with the death of a child, sandwiched between how to change diapers and the best way to blow their little noses. No handy tip can help you manage that much pain, her pain and ours.

I should have spent the next weeks hugging her tight and counting her toes, painting her little stomach purple and nibbling her ears. But I couldn't. I knew I'd never get over it.

There was blame to go around for everyone: the doctor, the neighbour, Simon, her genes, the way I'd cradled her as a newborn, those vegetables from the roadside stand. Me. It always came back to me.

Naming a billion guilty parties didn't make her whole. I was in pain, and Simon too, but she was singing. She tried to whistle but it just sputtered all over us. She pirouetted as she blew into her harmonica so we could admire her polka-dot dress. She faced down evil and death the way a child faces life and the future, oblivious to what it means but still making the most of it. It's different for us, those of us far too old to adapt.

Our friends and families were sad too. Everyone felt sorry for us. But no one suffered like we did, down to the very marrow of our bones. That's the part that was so hard to accept. Where did they get off smiling at us, asking how we were? One by one we pushed them out of our lives – because they hadn't suffered enough, because we needed to be left alone, the three of us, for these final months, this unfathomably brutal fight.

I remember one night, when we'd been sleeping for two hours, but she just wouldn't stop coughing and we all crawled into her little bed, Simon, her, and I, and we held back our tears all night so she would feel the warmth of our bodies and our caresses in her hair and our kisses on her skin.

Forty-five years from now, we'll remember this night, Simon whispered to me. I believed him.

⌒

I don't touch the gun. I've never told Simon, but ever since we lost our daughter I've had a recurring dream where I kill someone.

It might be a young man I don't know, ideally an unhappy young man who is battered and bruised and old beyond his years, though for obvious reasons I'd want his parents to still love him. They're the ones I have a bone to pick with. All the parents who've never known my pain and deserve a little taste. But I'm not strong enough, nor am I the type who can pull the trigger. I'm not even the type that reaches out and touches a firearm.

When I leave the shed, I'm all sweaty and my knuckles are white from an anger that will never dissipate, that makes my chest swell up from time to time. Simon isn't on his chaise longue. He didn't say where he was going. To the grocery store maybe. We often go out without telling each other where. Just out for a walk, to get away for a few minutes. Every time, I fear he won't come back. The two of us have been fighting the good fight together for so many years that I'd be defenceless if he stayed away too long.

I'm thirsty.

From the kitchen, just in front of the sink, I hear the ceiling creaking. Steps padding over the same square foot of flooring upstairs. I go up. Simon has his hand on my cello case, in the upstairs hallway. He's pacing back and forth like a sleepwalker, a madman, a metronome. Every few seconds his hand slips from the hinge of the case, only to return to it in the next second. He doesn't see me.

'What are you doing?'

Without really snapping out of his torpor, he stops pacing and turns to look at me. He's disappointed.

'I don't know. I … I don't know.'

He casts his eyes down. I stare at his hand, which keeps massaging the cello case. The memory of his thumb caressing my palm stabs me; I shiver. I take his other hand, the way you might grab a leash, and pull him toward the bedroom. He fights back. I pull him harder. We need to rest, need warmth, need each other's body. We need sex, a little taste of the life we had before. He's still resisting.

'No, Marie.'

He goes back over to the cello. I'm mad now. My anger is unfounded yet fierce. My voice is cracking, the blood rushing to my head.

'Stop it, Simon. Stop it.'

I drag him toward our bed and, try as he may to resist, I'm not having it. Twice he'll try to get off the mattress, and I'll pull him by the wrist, leaving marks I'll notice a few hours later. He'll try to push me away, but anger's always stronger than sadness, and he'll relent and close his eyes while I undress him. Later I'll imagine that he liked the roughness of it, found a way to get into the mood, was powerless to resist my mouth and hands on his skin. I imagined that in bed he could somehow share in my suffering and my desire, the dark urges driving me like furies. But after he comes, he looks troubled and scared, and the bruises on his chest that I'll only find tomorrow, along with his swollen lip from my biting, and his silence, his silence, will eloquently prove me wrong.

'I'm sorry, Simon.'

He stares at the ceiling and doesn't answer. Gangrenous from the shame of it, I get dressed and run out of the room and down the stairs, and yank the door open as if someone were chasing me. I have to run away. I run along the sidewalk of the main road. There's a blister on my heel, a fire burning my throat. My heartbeat is louder than my footsteps.

I ran until I could see skyscrapers. A bridge. The city. I passed through whole neighbourhoods whose existence I'd never guessed at. Got whistled at, sworn at, pushed around. When the first snowflakes landed on the asphalt, I saw my skin turn blue and felt my blood thicken. A snowplow grazed my shoulder. The sidewalk salt burned my feet, but I kept running. I slowed down when I recognized a house on the corner, with blue shutters, its staircase a different shade of blue. I caught my breath in the storm. In the distance a car struggled to clear a snowbank, while its wheels refused to co-operate. A man swore. The sun was back, its reflection on the snow crystals blinding. I slowed down so they wouldn't see me, so I wouldn't terrify them. The women next to me recognized me despite my scarf and the dissipating clouds and the steel-blue sky and the distant midday moon that has not changed in a million years. What a beautiful day, I said to myself, what a beautiful day. I crouched behind an ash tree to watch it unfold.

Since winter started, this was their favourite weekend ritual. They took their time getting dressed. Picked out her clothes together, though she always got the last word, even when she had no idea what she was pointing at, and laughing with her sharp little laugh that rose up from the deepest depths of her lungs. He always tickled her tummy before putting on her red one-piece snowsuit and tickled her toes before the boots went on. Then the nape of her neck before winding her scarf. Just when she couldn't contain her joy another second, they'd go out and face the cold, scrunching their eyebrows up like the world's most beautiful coureurs de bois. They never knew that I bundled up as well, and followed them at a distance, every time.

They made drawings in the blanket of snow, and on cars. Ran around. She took refuge in her father's arms, pretending to be too tired to walk. He was happy to lift her up. Then they'd go back to the park. It was their little secret: the only swing the city had forgotten to take down for the winter.

He'd push her on that swing for entire days and nights, and she didn't want to get off as long as she lived, and he didn't ever want to stop pushing. And I watched them, smiling up at the heavens, making the snow melt all around them and the tulips grow. At those times they were beauty itself.

~

Marie left me on the mattress like the unwanted dregs of a meal. I try to forget what just happened, but I can't. I'm cold. I put my old clothes back on – who cares if they're dirty – and go back to the cello. I wish I could burn it, but I won't.

Pushed by the need to get away from the instrument, from the bed, from here, I go out through the front door Marie didn't bother closing behind her. Her footprints are visible in the dirt alley. She was running. On the sidewalk, bouquets of weeds are sprouting up in the cracks. A car speeds by and disappears. A Chrysler maybe? It's loud and it's green. On the street corner Anne-Benedict is striding toward the next intersection in an emerald-green track suit with a blue terry-cloth headband. Before I can hide, she sees me and comes over. She's loud and she's green.

'Siiiiiiimon.'

Marie told me Anne-Benedict knows we don't like her. If that's true, she's playing it close to her chest.

'You're *just* the person I need to talk to!'

'I'm kind of busy – '

'It won't take long. I just wanted to say that … I wasn't clear with Marie the other day. I wanted to tell you guys that I really like you a lot. I don't care what you think of us – '

'Yeah, but we – '

'We like you guys.'

'That's nice.'

'And we really think once we get to know each other … it'll *totally* work. So you guys should just drop by. Any time. And get ready for the *royal treatment*.'

'Okay. Thanks.'

'And if you want to give us a little *heads-up*, just a day or two, so I can clean the house, that'd be even better!'

'Got it.'

'Well, we're totally looking forward to it! Want to come for a walk? It's a *terrific* way to stay in shape!'

I tell her I can't because I pulled a muscle falling down the stairs, a claim I illustrate by pointing at my chewed-up lip. Anne-Benedict walks off, panting.

I set off to check out the town, as I'd planned to do two months earlier. I feel the need to pretend everything is normal, as if the last few weeks and the last few hours had never been. I walk down the road and through the town's few streets, like a prospector on the hunt for nothing much. The streets are deserted, but the village still breathes. I peer into houses: a TV here, a green plant there – I'm looking for something. I'm not just trying to forget what happened in bed with Marie, or to get out of my house; I'm searching for someone to talk to. The kind of person I could tell my full story to and be sure they wouldn't hear a word of it. I don't want anyone to know that we fled the city, want to have a child, lost our daughter. They don't need to know about how we hurt each other and tell each other lies. But I need to tell someone. I'm looking for Alice.

The little grocery store is closed, so I keep going all the way to the tavern. Linda of the red hair and fair skin is behind the bar. She doesn't even look at me when I come in. I walk over to her. She puts a big open Labatt 50 down in front of me.

'Oh, no. I didn't want to – I just have a question.'

'Yeah, well, it's open now.'

I take a sip, to be polite. It doesn't go down right. My lower lip hurts, but I don't let it show. I'm trying to catch Linda's eye, but she's more interested in her crossword than my questions. The place is empty, the floor clean.

'I've got a question.'

'Yeah, you mentioned that,' she says.

'Can I … Can I ask you my question?'

'I don't know.'

'Because I've been looking. Well … I'm looking.'

'You won't find much here.'

'I'm looking for Alice. Where does she live?'

Linda finally raises her eyes and looks me square in the eye. I can read the displeasure in her lashes.

'Why?'

'I want to have a talk with her.'

'It's not like she's gonna listen. She's deaf. Mute too.'

'I know. But still.'

'Bad idea. Didn't you have a girlfriend, last time I checked? Go talk to her. And leave the rest of us alone.'

My patience is wearing thin. These people's fear of outsiders is grating on me.

'How about you just tell me where she lives?'

'Third house that way. Go ahead and knock: she won't hear you anyway. And don't say I didn't warn you. It's a bad idea, man.'

Linda of the red hair and increasingly florid complexion gives me her most disapproving look, and I walk out without paying. After all, I saved Patrick's life. I must have a few beers left on my tab.

The third house over looks much like every other house in town: dirty windows, rickety porch, complete silence.

I knock on the door. Footsteps. Alice opens, as if she'd been expecting me. She waves me in and points to a chair in the kitchen. While she's closing the door, I think I see the hint of a smile cross her face.

'The waitress at the bar said you wouldn't hear me if I knocked.'

'I heard you.'

❧

Near the end, just before she went into the hospital for good, our daughter figured out that I'd let her get away with anything. All manner of silliness, accidents, mischief: all it would ever take was an 'I didn't mean to' and we'd hug her and tell her it was no big deal. Marie and I reached an unspoken consensus. What was the point of spending our final moments together struggling to teach her life lessons and values she'd never get to put to use.

One Sunday she screamed in pain so loudly that the neighbour knocked to make sure we didn't need help. She screamed so loudly, as if from such terrible pain, that we both ran over. We found her holding her stomach and making a horrible face. When Marie stroked her hair, she started laughing, and laughing some more, and then she told us it was all a joke. She kept telling us over and over again. We didn't move, didn't tell her the story of the little boy who cried wolf. My hand on her stomach, Marie's on her head. From that moment on, we never knew whether her suffering was real or make-believe. And we didn't care.

❧

Alice sits across from me, worrying a strand of blond hair like a naughty child caught red-handed.

'No one knows anything except you, Simon. Everyone around here thinks I'm deaf. And it's for the best.'

'But why … ?'

'Want a cup of tea? I made tea.'

'What, did you know I was coming?'

'Maybe.'

She serves tea. I don't know what to think.

'I'm a local girl. Born and bred. Went to that boarded-up school. Back when there were still glass panes in the windows. But now, this town and everyone in it, it's all … For a young person like me, it's the worst place in the world. I left when I was sixteen, moved to the city. Just after they put the antenna in. I was there three years. Bad years. I ended up on the streets, running with a really sketchy bunch of people. When I got back here, I needed a fresh start, so I wrote something on a piece of paper. That I'd had an accident that had left me deaf and mute. People here aren't hard to fool, they believed me. They even gave me this house, but then that's not saying much. There are plenty of empty houses around here.'

'But why? Why would you make up something like that?'

'So I wouldn't have to talk to anyone. And so, when I go to get some rest, at the antenna … I like it that no one comes to bother me.'

'Yeah, sorry about that. I was kind of talking a lot out there.'

'Yeah.'

'What about now, though? How come you're willing to talk to me now?'

'Because you're really not doing well.'

Alice is telling me her story, as if faking deafness is just some joke I'll get a chuckle out of forty years from now. I almost want to call her on it. There's no excuse, it's not like she's living out her final months.

'You can't do that. You can't just lie like that.'

'Why not? They deserve it.'

'What did they ever do to you?'

'They destroyed me. I don't like them at all. I don't like people, period.'

'Sure, but what about values? How can you just make up a story like that?'

'It seemed funny at the time.'

'That's not funny. It's ridiculous.'

'Sweet. Here come the insults. See why I'd rather be a deaf-mute?'

'Want to know what I think? You're scared. You don't like people. And you're just too scared to deal.'

Up to now Alice has retained a hint of a smile in the corner of her mouth. Now her eyes cloud over. I've hit a nerve.

'You don't know me.'

She's right. I don't push my luck. My tea is lukewarm. The kitchen tap drips.

'You should ask Fisher to come fix it.'

'Yeah, I should.'

'Yeah.'

'Did you have something to tell me? Or did you just come here to stare at me some more?'

'Yeah, I wanted to talk to you. But that was when I thought you wouldn't hear me.'

❧

I spent a long time staring at the abandoned swing set behind an aspen tree in the town park, waiting for Simon, who never showed up. Though I knew he wouldn't come, I kept on waiting anyway, to apologize one more time, or maybe to yell at him again, or hit him even. Mostly, though, I wanted to ask his forgiveness. Then I dragged my feet through the sand in the play park, and jumped, and ran, and dug. I swung on the swings and slid down the slide, and I spun on the merry-go-round, full-tilt, singing away. I wanted to leave a trace that people would see, even if no one in this town would ever walk by this place after I left. I wanted footsteps turned up in the sand, so people would think there was still life going on here, that this dying village was still full of life.

I climbed up the little metal ladder one last time, all the way to the top, and sat there like the queen of the world. There was no one else there. Just the traces of my footsteps, my hands, in the sand below, and I knew all too well it wasn't children who had made them. The idea that not a single child would use this park again gave me the shivers.

Glimmers of the July sun were visible in the forest to the west. My perch was giving me vertigo. It might have been a lack of oxygen, up ten rungs above the ground, but I was short of breath. My head spun. I massaged my temples, but it didn't help. My pills were at home.

When I was a kid I used to black out a lot, and the first sign that it was coming was always a feeling of vertigo much like this. Back then I just had too much swirling around in my head. Too many words, too many ideas. But this afternoon is different. The problem is there's nothing left in my mind except the fear that I've reached the end of the road.

The tips of my fingers feel like a swarm of insects is gnawing away underneath my nails. I can't feel my feet anymore – yet there they are, I see them. I let myself go, fall down. My body slides down the burning metal and I collapse into the sand, the desert sand of the Mariana Trench, and after that I don't remember anything at all.

When I come to, it'll be dark.

His lips on my forehead, a tender kiss. The smell of liquor. I open my eyes. There's sand under my fingernails. I hope it's Simon kissing me, but it's not. It's Fisher. He's holding me with one arm and caressing me with the other.

'You scared me. I was scared you were … This slide is dangerous. You shouldn't come to this park. You shouldn't – '

'I want to go home.'

'Sure. I'll take you. What happened?'

What can I tell him? That I played in the park until I collapsed from fatigue, or disgust? That the queens of the world never hold on to their crowns long? He holds out a bottle. I drink. The cheap whisky feels like it will tear out my gums and strip every pipe clean. I cough. It's the first time in weeks that the tears in my eyes are not tears of rage.

'Gets the heart started, hey?'

'I've had better.'

'I'll have to bring the wine list next time.'

'It's fine. Thanks, Fisher.'

'No one ever comes to this park. I couldn't miss you.'

'Thanks. Could you take me home now?'

'You sure there's nothing else I can do for you?'

'No, that's fine. I just need to go to bed. Sleep until the winter, I think.'

'I could keep you warm.'

'I've got everything I need at home.'

Last time we met, his indifference bothered me; this time, his proximity repels me.

'Sure, I'll take you home. Just promise me one thing.'

'What's that?'

'Don't ever come to this park again. It's a bad place.'

I silently agree. Fisher's old truck will weave its way down the road to our house. While I make my way from his truck to the front door, Fisher will stare at the house as if he'd seen a ghost in the window. I'll forget to thank him and go take four pills. I'll take refuge in bed, where Simon's arms will be waiting and will clasp me in silence as if tonight were just another night. I'll love him more than ever, but I'll wait until he's sleeping to say sorry.

I saw Eddie again a few years ago, far from the weather station by our childhood home. The passage of time and the pop-psychology articles I'd skimmed over the years had convinced me that being punched by me all those years ago marked his psyche. His thirst for revenge must have been transformed into a passion for weightlifting. Of course, my interpretation was based on nothing more substantial than the need to believe that my every action touched people's lives, that though I may not leave physical traces of my passage on this earth, I would at least leave behind formative memories that inspired everyone I encountered to rise to greater heights. Yeah, I was young and naive.

Eddie was in his mid-twenties when I saw him again. He rolled up in his wheelchair, and I imagined I was about to be treated to the benefits of hard-won wisdom born of suffering. I was wrong. The moment he recognized me, he sped over to me, braked at my feet, and spat on the ground.

'If I could stand up, I'd break that pretty face of yours. Teach you to mind your own business.'

Then he turned around and sped off into the distance. I stood there a good long while. My only legacy was the memory of that childhood act of violence.

Years later, when we lost our daughter and I was looking hard for a silver lining at the bottom of a bottle, I thought about Eddie. It made me see it didn't really matter that she hadn't lived long enough to make her mark. At least she hadn't done perma-nent damage to anyone, the way her father had left this man scarred for life. Then I decided this was the very saddest thought

I could think, and I felt guilty. She never got the chance to create memories, write pitiful love letters, carve her name in the wood of a picnic table, break a window. She never got to be hated, or to be loved, or to punch someone who would never forgive her for it.

⤚

I die a small death each and every time I think of her short life. Today, in our backyard, I almost died. I was trying to find the box we'd put her urn in. Bad idea. I tore strips of cardboard off dozens of boxes, with no real desire to find the entirety of her earthly remains packed into a lifeless vessel. But I kept looking anyway. I stopped when I found a photo of Marie. She's smiling and happy. A photo from before. I closed the boxes as best I could and spread out on a chaise longue in the yard. My head felt heavy. I tried to find a way to slow the death creeping through my veins.

Behind our backyard there's a forest, a sort of partition wall between people and the unknown, with a path so narrow it must be years since anyone walked down it. Twenty inches of grass unreachable by lawn mower – that is, if we ever took it upon ourselves to mow the lawn – stand between me and the path, me and the forest.

For weeks I've been observing this passage. I'm drawn to it, terrified of it. I don't think Marie has ever noticed it, and I'm not about to mention it to her. Today, to lose myself, I'm going to go check out the path.

On the other side of the tall grass lies a black forest. I enter a void of trees and leaves. The August wind doesn't blow here. The birds, if there are birds here, remain silent. I have to bend my back and clench my arms against my sides, kneel on the ground, and lean my head, and even with all these contortions I still scrape my brow. A branch nicks my eyelid; a root attacks my ankle. Nature is contracting all around me, engulfing and strangling me, then relinquishing me for a moment before contracting further. I set off, push forward, and finally slip through to the other side and into the vast, cavernous forest.

If our daughter were with me, she would see the thousands of spiderwebs between the trees, and I would kiss her neck and lift her up so she wouldn't scrape her knee. I stand still here on the other side, as great drafts of humidity waft over me, and it's her smile on my face. My aunts were wrong: she never looked like me. I was the one who looked like her.

The birds up high, their beating wings. That rustling of feathers under quivering bodies, gentle as a mother's cooing. Something is enfolding me. It feels like in these woods I've finally found the peace of mind I've been searching for since I closed my eyes. Haphazardly, slowly, I make my way forward. As I brush the leaves, amniotic drops tickle my skin.

I embrace the freedom of getting lost, breathing in the dust from the branches and the insects and the rain imprisoned under strata of last autumn's leaves. Daytime is as dark as nighttime here. And I'm at peace.

This old abandoned path feels more like home to me than our house behind it. Every footfall wrings the moisture from old leaves still waterlogged from yesterday's drizzle. I move forward on wet toes, going nowhere. It's like swimming through an organism so much larger than ourselves, with no other purpose than to discover the forgetting and to search for an empty nook to crawl into, waiting for nature to forgive me.

Even on a scorching August day, it's like winter in this coal forest. It's actually cold. Under the evergreens are millions of insects, and under the deciduous trees there is me. Below me a river, at a standstill. I can see its eroding banks, and the path it has cut. It had conviction once, but the water doesn't move anymore. I throw a branch, which could float for hours without moving. Large concentric ripples reach the bank, then disappear.

I cross the river with my feet in the water, submerged to my waist, but when I come out on the other side my clothes are dry. On this bank the carpet of pine needles is softer than lace, and the ferns tickle my calves. In the distance there's a pink glow, between the tree trunks, to the east. Stifled laughter. A neon sign.

~

I often used to rest in the old broken rocking chair that belonged to my great-grandmother. We'd put it in the corner of our daughter's bedroom, and during nap time I'd go watch her sleep, until I joined her in dreamland. When she'd wake up crying, I'd pretend I hadn't slept at all.

It was an autumn night and we didn't yet know she was sick, but she must have been. Marie had told her the story of the sheep with the big silver curls who thought he was so handsome. I'd kissed her on the left earlobe, like I did every night. I whispered that I'd see her in my dreams, and we'd left the room. She started coughing, and then crying, and I tried to get her to sleep on my own, in vain. Marie and I would take turns coming into her room just to watch her sleep. Sometimes we'd stroke her face a little, or whisper a few sweet words. Then Marie took out her cello and set it up in her room. I sat in the rocking chair. It felt as if she played all night. I wanted it never to end. Our girl was fighting off sleep, so she wouldn't miss a single note. The pain was gone. She was smiling. It's the expression on her face as she marvelled at the music from Marie's cello that I'll hold in my memory, forever.

❧

Between the trees, ants dance. Mosquitoes too, and farther off, a fox perhaps, and even a coyote. Every step brings me closer to the neon sign and the building it's affixed to. It's framed by the trees, accessible by neither road nor path. I see no power lines to feed its dazzling neon sign: 'BOWLING ALLEY – OPEN 24 HOURS.' From outside, the building looks abandoned. Ivy has grown over the brick, the foundation stone is crumbling away, and a tree trunk has pushed over one of the walls. An upper-floor window is broken. Three bricks are missing. A flower has taken root in the mortar. The gutter's rusted out. From inside, I can hear a cheerful hum.

Since I crossed the river, I've been walking through a forest blanketed in invisible fog and smelling of popcorn. I open the door. I haven't been bowling since I was twelve. It was my birthday. My parents and all my friends were there. I remember we ate hot dogs.

The door creaks like it hasn't been opened since the invention of the hinge. In the cloakroom, plants have broken through the floor. Proliferating mushrooms, an empty bird's nest, footprints all over the dirt floor. A second door appears, nothing like the first: polished metal as shiny as a mirror, with a new doorknob.

This second door has attitude, and it's taunting me, just daring me to push. *C'mon, open me!* I don't hold out long.

The moment I step onto the burgundy carpet, there is no past. In this sparkling bowling alley, it's an eternal present. Twenty or so people are sitting around having a gay old time. My ears fill up with the joyful melodies coming from the speakers, and I try to find a path through the players' laughter and the heavenly clacking of upended bowling pins. I need a hot dog.

Behind the canteen counter, a long-haired twenty-year-old guy douses my frank in mustard and covers everything in a small mountain of sauerkraut. The coloured lights along the back wall make me dizzy. I close my eyes and bite into the most delicious mustard-sauerkraut hot dog in human history. The steamed bun and cheap wiener taste like happiness and hope.

In lane three the game is heating up. A seventy-year-old in a tuxedo is in a hard-fought match with his ten-year-old grandson. When the kid throws a gutter ball, his face is transformed into pure disappointment. The old man sees his opportunity and takes it: he purposely misses his final throw, to keep the score close. When the boy sees the mustard stain on my chin, he bursts into laughter, but his grandfather reminds him to be polite, and that serious look comes over his face again. I wink at him to show him I'm not bothered. He winks back, and I notice that he has different-coloured eyes: his right is blue, his left is brown. Behind them I sense something serene.

'I wear a nine-and-a-half,' I tell the nearly bald old lady at the shoe counter. She digs around and pulls out a pair of bowling shoes: blue, white, and brown. In these I'll be the Don Juan of this bowling alley. A gentle giant with a persistent cough invites me to join his game. I don't play hard to get, and I grab a big ball in the same colours as my shoes. I bowl. Goddamn gutter ball. I laugh.

Then a little girl, who couldn't be much older than six, runs down to the farthest lane. She breaks into peals of laughter that make her hair shake and transform her face. One of her sandals is unbuckled. I watch her enjoying herself for two or three or maybe ten hours, but I can't approach. I don't dare, afraid I'll realize she's not our daughter. But it is her, it has to be; it's her I'm sitting here admiring without feeling a crack in my bones or a knife in my blood. No dizziness.

The music grows louder and more overpowering. Across the room, a woman is dancing. I tap my foot along with the Bob Marley. In this bowling alley in the middle of the forest, I've finally found the place where I belong. The kid with the different-coloured eyes gives me a wave. I close my eyes. It's raining.

～

I haven't shared my sylvan adventures with Marie, and she wouldn't believe me anyway. But the scene remains imprinted on my memory, and I know the day will come when I'll want to go back there. This time I'll hit my 4–10 split, and the giant in the bowling alley will clap. And I'll get to hear my daughter's burbling laugh again.

'What's up with you?' asks Marie.

'Nothing. Why?'

'You look way too happy.'

'I'm in a good mood, that's all. You should give it a try.'

'Sure. Just show me how.'

I hold a hand out toward Marie, but she doesn't have time to take it before Anne-Benedict marches through our house and out the back door, straight into our yard. Though she looks mad, we're unable to hide our amusement.

'Yeah, laugh it up! At my expense.'

'What's going on here? You look – '

'I'm pissed, that's what. All we want is a nice life, a nice life with our friends. But then what do our "friends" go and do? They never come over, even though they're invited. What are you waiting for? The first snow?'

We learned two things that afternoon. One: even perfect people get mad. And two: Anne-Benedict considers us her friends, which is amusing. But our remaining shred of decorum helps us hide our true feelings.

'We're sorry, Anne. We wanted to visit you. There's just a lot going on right now. In our personal lives.'

'You know, we have one too. A personal life, that is. It doesn't stop us from going out and seeing people.'

'I – '

'But even hearing you say that you want to come see us, it makes me want to … wipe the slate clean.'

Wow, Anne-Benedict is giving us a clean slate. However will we contain our joy?

'The kids have whipped up a little something for you too. So don't wait too long.'

'Is it an ashtray?'

'Of course not, don't be silly. You don't smoke. It's a surprise!'

She claps. We clap back in the hope that that will send her on her merry way. Surprise: it doesn't. She'll spend the next couple hours telling us all about her wonderful children, who sound able to do just about everything that every other child their age can do. We'll congratulate her, again and again. Because we're friends.

When she finally leaves, we'll hold one another in silence for a full minute and bask in the miraculous power Anne-Benedict exercises over our relationship.

'I love you, Simon.'

I start clapping. She pushes me away with a laugh.

⟋

That morning we drove all the way into the city and back without bursting into tears. Small victories. We bought gas and oil for the lawn mower, determined to attack the boreal jungle of our lawn, once and for all. Before firing up the lawn mower, Simon looks up at me.

'Are we doing this now?'

'Later.'

Simon is sweating profusely, despite the cool early-autumn weather, as he endeavours to clear our overgrown yard, which feels more like a garden maze. He's progressing at a rate of one inch per hour, it seems, though he's adept at inventing excuses.

'I'm taking it slow. You know, in case there are hidden bears.'

By lunchtime Simon has mowed what looks like one square foot of lawn. We bought a croquet set this morning, to reward us for doing some work.

'C'mon, mow. I can't wait to kick your ass.'

'You'll never beat me.'

He keeps mowing, purposely taking his time, either to make me wait or to get a rise out of me. I don't care. I pretend to concentrate on my croquet strokes, but it's a struggle not to embrace sloth on such a lovely day.

'Do you want to do it now?' he asks.

'Let's wait a bit, okay?'

We play half a game – just enough to remind us that we both really don't like croquet. Our duel is interrupted when Simon misses an easy shot and throws his mallet into the forest. I hold him tight, pretending to be angry. We fall to the ground. I hurt my elbow, but Simon's kisses soothe me. We let the time go by, spread out on the Kentucky bluegrass clippings with white clover mixed in.

An hour goes by, then another. We're far away from our chaise longues, far away from these past months, and far away from her as well. We suddenly wake up at quarter past five. I put on my most serious expression, though I can feel a roiling in my blood. He knows.

'I think I'm ready.'

He nods, and we go into the house. There's no doubt in my mind: I'm pregnant. I know it. It's the kind of thing you just know, even before shutting yourself up in the bathroom with some fancy pregnancy test.

It's our best day since we moved here. Simple, and sweet, with the smells of gasoline and motor oil and massacred greenery and love. A child. This will be our last good night here.

～

Tomorrow the town's little store will close its doors for good. I'm surprised to discover that, although we have no need of groceries, I want to go in and say goodbye to the owner.

'You should mind your own business,' says Simon. 'They've made that much clear.'

'Yeah, but I like the store owner. And I feel bad for him. He loves this little town so much.'

'Why's he leaving then?'

I don't know. Maybe I'll ask him. Or maybe I'll just kiss him on the cheek and wave goodbye.

The little store has been emptied of its wares, along with its customers. All that's left is the old grocer, standing motionless behind his counter. He looks eager to postpone his departure. I have no doubt that if he could he'd stand there, without moving an inch, for a few years more. He smiles at me.

'You're that guy's wife! I'm going to miss you … '

'You too. It's funny, hey?'

'Yeah. I'm not the kind of guy who really likes people, but you … you're all right! Of course, I don't really know you. Maybe that's why.'

'I'm pregnant.'

I have no idea why I feel the need to share my news with him. An excess of enthusiasm, or a moment of misguided emotion. Either way, his reaction is not what I had in mind. His smile vanishes. He looks terrified.

'Whatever you do, don't stay here. Get the hell out of here! Go back to the city. This is a bad place for kids. The devil's here.'

I hope he's kidding and let out a hearty laugh. But he doubles down and my smile fades.

'I'm not joking. You have to get out of here. This is a bad place … '

'Is that why you're leaving?'

'No, for me it's … another story.'

'You can tell me. It's not like we're ever going to see each other again.'

'I'm leaving because Madeleine doesn't love me. I still had some hope, but it's clear to me now. We talked. I've been waiting for her for three years. And now I know nothing will ever happen between us.'

'Three years?'

'Madeleine was married to Big Bert. The guy who had the grocery store before me. I guess that's why I never liked him. I've been in love with her for twenty years, and when Big Bert left us, I figured that … If I took over the grocery store … It's dumb, I know. But I needed to believe in something. Ever since they put the antenna in, people around here stopped believing in anything at all. I just wanted to believe in something.'

'And now you don't anymore … '

'No.'

'And that's why you're leaving?'

'Yeah. And you should too.'

'But we came here to have a baby.'

'Bully for you. Knock yourselves out. Just don't say I didn't warn you.'

'What's going on here anyway? What happened?'

'Lots of stuff, and none of it's your business. Remember how I told you that everyone hated the old guy? Everyone has their reasons. Well, ask Fisher. Ask Fisher what his reasons are.'

❧

Simon's wearing Christian's skin-tight bathing suit and trying in vain to hide it behind his beer bottle. I'm wading in the Lavoies' pool next to Anne-Benedict, wondering what the hell we're doing here. In a moment of confusion, drunk on the positive pregnancy test, Simon had the ingenious idea of inviting ourselves for a dip in the Lavoies' chlorinated pool.

'We owe them a visit, right?'

'I guess so.'

'And, you know … they are the only other family in town. It wouldn't be the worst thing in the world to get friendly with them, right?'

'Yeah. Sure.'

It's true that we don't like the Lavoies. But it's equally true that, throughout those dark days of summer, we didn't exactly give them much of a chance. Which is why, this afternoon, Simon and I solemnly swore to believe in the possibility of friendship. When we rang the doorbell, our enthusiasm was genuine. And the moment Anne-Benedict opened, we immediately regretted our decision. She feigns annoyance for a fraction of a second, then starts beating her wings and chirping. Before we can even say hi, she's run over to the sideboard, clapping her hands, and brought over two papier-mâché rabbits. The kids' surprise for us. We smile, show a little tooth.

The pool is as tepid as our conversation. Out of politeness, or just laziness, we pretend to enjoy Anne-Benedict's stories.

'Delphine changed daycares two weeks ago. It's tough! She doesn't want to take her nap anymore.'

'Ah.'

'Patrick's totally better now!'

She must be wilfully ignoring the little kicks and clenched fists, nervous tics her son didn't seem to have at the beginning of the summer. But his teacher has nothing but good things to say. He's 'a little fireball,' and 'always ready to join right in,' so Anne-Benedict feels good.

'I never told you about my name, I guess?'

'No, I don't think so.'

'I hate "Benedict." I always ask people to just call me Anne.'

'Why don't you like it? It's not so bad … '

'I just don't like eggs!'

'Huh?'

'That's all. I never liked eggs Benedict.'

I pretend to understand why she's sharing this tidbit with us, while struggling to conceal my boredom. Even Simon, who would normally have found this little anecdote amusing, appears to be at a loss. At least we have papier-mâché rabbits to cheer us up.

I had been planning to tell the Lavoies I was pregnant. But the more this day goes by, the less I feel like it. I don't dare talk to Simon about it. He looks happy, but even back in the bathroom I had to wonder. The day after I told him, it rained, and just like every time, the rain brought back the memory of our daughter, and I imagined he was coming to tell me that nothing could ever replace her, that she'd never relinquish her place for another child. Since then, that's all I can think about. I'm haunted by the fear that we've finally achieved our goal, but it was the wrong goal; we've been working toward the wrong goal all along.

Today at the Lavoies', in the throes of an emotionally painful bout of vertigo, my doubts are confirmed. I'll never be a mother again. The mere sight of Simon enjoying himself with someone else's child is odious to me. The carelessness of the Lavoies, who don't even bother keeping an eye on their little rug rats, horrifies me. I could never.

For three years I worried day and night about things that would never happen to her. In nightmares I agonized over each detail of her life up to age one hundred: I fretted over her adolescence, her first love and starting school and her big mean neighbour and travelling and drugs and her first apartment in a sketchy neighbourhood and sexually transmitted diseases and her shyness and her first car crash and her sick cat and the eight times her heart would break. Her grief at our funerals, when Simon and I die. I've known these fears, and these nightmares are still vivid to me. I know she'll never face any one of these things, and still I must experience them, one by one.

My big girl should have lived a normal life with the standard allotment of hardship spread over a lifetime, instead of those three months of nuclear holocaust suffering, that condensed version comprised entirely of pain with all the pleasure hollowed out. No ceasefires, just battles. My very own big girl deserved to be protected from everything I could shelter her from, all those things we should have fought off together, all three of us together finding peace and keeping it.

My life sentence is to live out my days fearing for someone who's found a place where she's untouchable.

And I'll be a thousand times more fearful for the next child, the one clinging to the insides of my uterus, multiplying and growing inside me. My fears will run the gamut. Fear of sickness. No, I can't. I had an abortion when I was seventeen, and I promised myself never again. And I won't do it ever again. But I also won't be capable of watching this child grow up.

We'll be the worst parents in the world. The kind that miss the one they lost and so forever stifle the one who's there with them. And we'll hate ourselves for it.

～

Marie can't hide the violet spot deep in her eye. She can't keep her sadness hidden anymore. She thinks I'm happy, but I'm not. I've known for a long time that a new child won't fix a thing. I understood the first time I touched the antenna. I just never told Marie. I didn't want to single-handedly destroy our one dream of a future here. But I think she gets it now.

Doing such a bang-up job of pretending to be happy has at least provided me a sanctuary of sorts. All I have to do is close my eyes and the memory of the bowling alley appears, clear as day, along with the music and the yelling and all the other people. Her. But today, here in the yard with Patrick's soccer ball and Delphine's scooter, I'm vulnerable. I can see Marie teetering on the brink. We should really leave before we fall to pieces.

I put my beer bottle down on the picnic table. The Lavoies' lawn is magnificent, perfectly mown, without the slightest bulge cloaking the smallest imperfection. They're so hard to like. Anne-Benedict tiptoes over to me. I hope she's going to invite me to do some crafting.

'Can I talk to you, Simon?'

I wordlessly agree. She starts walking toward the house, and I realize I'm meant to follow her. In the thoroughly modern kitchen, my heart leaps up at the sight of a sinkful of dirty dishes. Anne-Benedict deliberately touches my arm before beginning her speech. It must be her way of achieving maximum awkwardness. I don't know what she wants to tell me. I won't tell her that I already don't care and am really only concerned about Marie, who's quietly losing her mind next to their pool.

'I'm not happy, Simon.'

' … '

'I'm just not happy. Did I tell you Christian cheated on me? Last summer. Some girl on set. It lasted two weeks, but it hurt. I doubt you can understand what that kind of hurt feels like.'

'Oh, I'm pretty sure I can.'

'Anyway, it broke me into a thousand pieces. But I couldn't bring myself to leave him. I just couldn't do it. I had to forgive him. I had no choice. I'm ashamed, but I just had no choice. I love him so much. And if I left him, it would have been me suffering. That's the worst thing when someone cheats on you. You're a double loser. If you want to punish the other person, you only hurt yourself. So I stayed. I forgave him.'

'It's okay to forgive, Anne. Forgiving is a good thing.'

'But I'm not happy. I can't forget. I just can't. Ever since the beginning of the summer I just can't stop thinking about it and telling myself I should leave him. But there are the kids to think about. Poor kids.'

'You have to find a way to be happy, Anne.'

'If you had any idea how ashamed I am … Sometimes I wish my kids would die. I'd never kill them, obviously. Don't worry about that! But I imagine it would be easier if they died in an accident. Then I could leave Christian. What should I do, Simon?'

There are so many couples staying together because they have kids. And Marie and I stay together because we don't. I'm oscillating between being depressed and wanting to give Anne-Benedict a good hard slap. But I'm not a violent guy. And she doesn't know better, because she doesn't know about our girl. She's never seen the urn tucked away in the moving box we'll never open. She doesn't know. We have to get out of here.

'What should I do, Simon?'

'Do it. Kill your kids. That'll make you happy, for sure.'

I walk out before she has the chance to inflict an answer on me, and I rejoin Marie by the pool.

We're on the sidewalk trying to recover our spirits when we come to a happy agreement: we'll simply stop talking to the Lavoies. Their soap-opera dramas can't touch us; there's nothing we can do for them. They'll serve out their sentence and keep pretending to be happy as they navigate their small sea of disappointments, and we'll just have to accept our fate and never again be privy to their tales of speed walking and papier-mâché. When we got home, our house felt calm, and we did our best to be happy in spite of it all. And for several days in a row we managed to be relatively happy. Then the rain came back.

Today big fat raindrops cascade down our windowpanes in torrents and streams. Simon is upstairs, playing Scrabble against himself. That way he's sure to win. It makes him feel better. I'm hanging out in the kitchen, watching the heavens pour forth onto our house. The sound is our daughter's emphatic reminder that she will always be here with us. The clouds are crying, the stars are shooting. Everything's ephemeral, all is at peace. And then the cold.

What I'm feeling isn't typical first-trimester fatigue. I'm familiar with that feeling – brutal yet tender, bitter yet sweet. What

I'm feeling now is too close to anger not to spark alarm. I suspect it might be too late. Or maybe too early. At any rate, my toe is wet. An oblong puddle on the floor is growing larger. Soon my feet will be encircled.

'Simon! It's leaking!'

We spend a while patting walls in an attempt to find the leak, before we realize its source is on the other side of the wooden door. The water heater. We can't say we weren't warned. We call the service station right away because fast-leaking water is an emergency. It's a conviction Fisher clearly doesn't share. He shows up four hours later, with an allegedly new tank in the back of his pickup and a steel cooler he has found the time to fill up with booze.

Fisher makes himself comfortable in the kitchen. He's in no earthly hurry. Empty beer bottles are stacking up, with no tangible sign of progress. Simon retreats to the bedroom to play 'quandary' with the 'q' on a triple letter score. It's a humiliating blow against his Scrabble alter ego, but I know full well he went upstairs more to get away from Fisher than to enjoy his solo game.

'Your husband doesn't like me much,' says Fisher, seven beers deep.

'Uhh. Yeah … '

'Makes sense. I'm not an easy guy to like.'

'Let's just say our first meeting was – '

'Yeah. I don't mind if he doesn't like me. I like him just fine.'

'Me too.'

I'm trying to keep conversation to a minimum. I don't want to distract Fisher more than is strictly necessary. He's drunkenly weaving as he pushes the dolly with the old tank on it. It's still raining outside, and the ground is slick. Fisher slips. Then he shoves the old tank, letting it fall where it may, and endeavours to unload the 'new' one from his truck. Simon joins me on the landing, with a raincoat on.

'Going out?'

'Yeah, I'm going for a walk.'

'Everything okay?'

'I … Yeah, you know me. I can't stand it when people promise you something, and then half-ass it. It makes me – '

'He'll figure it out.'

'I know he will. But right now it's just making me mad … I don't know … He's already missing a couple teeth … '

Simon has managed to make me smile. I place my mouth on his, to slow time down a notch. I don't mind if it takes eight years to change the water heater. I clench my lips and press them to his face. His hand slides onto my stomach, and I want to believe, at that very moment I so badly want to believe. A family of our own, a little brother or sister for her. With his hand on my stomach, I just have to believe.

'I … '

'Me too.'

❧

The gullies along the sidewalk are my guide. I feel bad for leaving Marie alone to manage this drunken DIY disaster, but I needed some fresh air. I walk as slowly as I can, dodging the raindrops bombarding me from above. The gullies turn left, and I follow them.

Dirty windows, decrepit porch. I knock on the door. No answer. I knock again, and then once more. Alice finally opens, with sleepy eyes and pillow marks on her face.

'What are you, deaf?'

She doesn't laugh, just gives me a shove that sends me stumbling down to the bottom of the porch stairs, and then closes the door. I'm left alone on the sidewalk. I don't move. I notice that no amount of rain can cleanse these windows of years of pollution from the factory and construction, smoke and dust and sputum. I take two steps toward home. Alice walks out the front door in a yellow raincoat that's too big for her. A hood covers her big black eyes. She wears kids' sandals on her feet.

'I feel like swinging. Let's go to the park.'

I'd rather go anywhere but there, but I don't hear any choices. Alice is already walking fast. I'm slowed by the clenching in my gut. The park. The kids who aren't there.

'Wait for me.'

Faithful to habit, she pretends not to hear me. When we get to the park, she sits on a swing and starts pushing with her feet, taking off her hood and facing the sky.

'We can talk here. No one ever comes to this park.'

'I noticed.'

'You don't like the park, hey?'

'Bad memories.'

'Is that why you're struggling? The bad memories?'

'I had a kid. A girl.'

'What was her name?'

I shake my head. Alice opens her mouth wide, to taste the rain.

'You should try drinking some rain. It'll make you feel better.'

'Maybe.'

'So do you miss your daughter?'

'Yeah. Lots. But it's getting better now.'

'Are you sure?'

'Sure. Marie's pregnant.'

'You know that no one can replace another person, right? It doesn't work that way.'

'I know.'

I'm not sure she understands. She's swinging higher and higher in the air, as if slipping the bonds of the gravity that governs our discussion.

'Congratulations, though.'

She abruptly stops swinging, with two feet in the sand and her sandals full of mud.

She's nineteen years old and has big black eyes and there are a thousand and one questions I really don't want to ask.

'You remind me of her,' I say. 'My daughter. A little older, though.'

'I'll take that as a compliment.'

'Yeah. She had your … gusto. That devil-may-care attitude. If she was your age, she'd be the kind of person who'd convince the entire world she's deaf and mute. I don't know how I know, but I'm sure of it.'

'I think I'd like your daughter.'

I open my mouth and taste the rain. The cold raindrops on my tongue in September out here in the country feel good.

'Feels good, hey?' says Alice.

'Yeah.'

'Told you so.'

'Know what? I like thinking that you're exactly the person my girl might have become.'

A darkness sweeps over Alice, and her eyes close. She nods, then shakes her head. Goes to say something, but doesn't. She gets off the swings and walks away. I follow her, at a distance. Then she comes back.

'Are you from the city or the country?' she asks me.

'The city.'

'Why here, then? Why'd you come here anyway? You must have known this town is dying. That there'll be nothing left in a year or two.'

'We didn't really think it through.'

Alice keeps walking, and we pass a few still-inhabited houses. She goes mute again. When I speak to her she doesn't turn around. The people sitting by their living-room windows can see me talking to her, I'm sure. They must think I'm crazy. Or that I don't know any better. When I get to her place, she pushes the door open and closes it, and I don't know if I should follow her in or not. I follow her in.

Alice has tossed her raincoat on the ground and is rummaging around in the fridge. She pulls out a bottle of Coke and doesn't offer me any. She looks me in the eye, and behind the barbed wire, in the dark depths of her pupils, I sense a sadness as deep as a well.

'If you think your daughter would have ended up like me, it's probably a good thing she died.'

&

We celebrated her third birthday at the hospital, a few weeks before she died. At that point she was crying more and more, and there was nothing we could do to console her. Opaque curtains, rust spots on the cast-iron pipe, beige stains on the suspended ceiling.

It was Tuesday.

She was suffering, and she was staring at me, and she was trying to tell me something; *you have to do something, you're my dad.*

But there was nothing I could do, and this made me suffer with her, and I couldn't let it show. She was lost, distraught, trying desperately to find the dad she knew, the one who up to now had always found a way to make her feel better. This time he didn't know what to do. She was crying and it was her birthday and we brought cake. The travesty of that cake haunts me to this day.

On that day I wanted death to come for her. You don't get over that. You serve out your sentence, condemned to crawl blindly through each and every day as they rise up like the steps on a never-ending stairway of shame, leaving a trail of blood and bile, and an echo of my screams. This life was like a long, drawn-out tooth extraction, as the hours following her death slowly disintegrated. On her sweat-soaked bed, the wheezing, the gasps of despair, I wished I could be deaf and blind. Her little hand in my big hand. Just a few months earlier we were still playing Count Your Fingers. But she won't remember any of it. I'm the one who'll be haunted by these memories. On Tuesday nights just after midnight all the three-year-olds in the world are sleeping in their little beds, but not her. I squeezed her hand just a little too hard and I thought, you're squeezing too hard, and I thought she'd be better off dead, she and I would both be better off, I thought, once we were over and done with this.

I'll never be able to live with the guilt that thought brings me still.

❧

Alice is waiting for an answer. I don't have one. I stare at the floor.

'Did you know that the house you bought is the one I grew up in?'

'No, I didn't know that ... '

'The old guy was my dad.'

'Really?'

'And you must know that he's the reason I had to get out of here?'

'Why?'

'Because he was ... uuuhhh ... '

'He was what?'

'Never mind.'

She looks down. I wait. She starts up again.

'When I was four, I used to play in the backyard with a friend my age. We liked digging up worms. One day he disappeared, but I was playing and didn't notice. His mom came over and started calling for him, but he didn't answer. She was yelling like a crazy person and shaking me, to make me tell her what had happened. I had no idea what happened. I hadn't seen a thing. They thought he'd gone to hide in the forest out back and spent days looking for him. They never found him. Do you know what happens in cases like that? People need a scapegoat. I was the only one around.'

'But you were four ... '

'I know. And they knew too. But in a little town like this, things happen fast, and before long everyone had made up their minds. My parents tried to protect me as best they could. But it was super-hard on them. My mom died not long after. Heart attack. It took a few years, but gradually people sort of forgot about me. But there's always been a little something that stuck. Let's just say no one around here ever really liked me.'

'Is that why you left town?'

'No.'

Alice puts her Coke bottle down on the table. Her hands are shaking, and she won't look me in the eye. Outside the rain has stopped and a ray of sun is doing its best to light up Alice's face, but she backs up her chair to stay out of its way.

'Three years ago, I was babysitting my brother's son. He was a real little daredevil. Like every six-year-old, I guess. I took him to the park, and he was jumping all over the place, running around, throwing sand at me. I was laughing my head off. We were having lots of fun, but at one point he started doing acrobatics on top of the fucking slide. I yelled at him to stop, that it was dangerous. That just made him go harder. And he fell. He landed really bad. Broke his neck. Literally. Paralyzed for life. And I cried – you have no idea how I cried.

'Of course, no one in the village saw that. All anyone saw was a paralyzed kid, and who was to blame? The same girl who'd caused the disappearance of the other kid, twelve years earlier. It was my fault again, except this time I wasn't four years old, I was sixteen. And it was my second time. Right away everyone could tell there was something not right about me. And this time, my dad wasn't standing up for me. He was so cut up about losing his grandson that he bought into the idea that it was my fault.

'After that, he started having episodes. He'd go through spells where he wasn't lucid, just for a while. I left just before he died. I didn't hear that he'd died until two years after it happened. That was when I came back.'

'Why'd you come back?'

'It's crazy, right? I chose to come back to this place where I'm the most hated person in the world. Does that give you any idea of how awful my life was in the city? Here … it's home. Here is where I want to make my life. So I've hidden away, in silence, it was easier that way. And I'm waiting. Not sure what for, but I'm waiting.'

'…'

'See what I'm saying? If your girl had turned out like me, she'd have this curse. Of making people disappear. And she'd be such a bad person you wouldn't even want to stick up for her.'

'But none of that was your fault.'

'I don't even know anymore.'

I shut my mouth. I sidle over like I'm approaching a wolf, eyes averted, scarcely moving, one millimetre at a time. She's crying. I hug her and she hugs me back. Her body's shaking. She is quaking in time to each sob. She holds me tight and I hold her tight.

'But I want things to get better. I want the same "better" you do.'

⌀

Fisher's pickup is still in our driveway. Night has fallen. The rain has stopped, and I can't chase the thought of Alice from my mind. Now I understand what gives her eyes that colour. I walk around the house to the back door. In the murky moonlight I feel the short-trimmed grass tickling my toes. Or maybe it's the ants.

It's dark in the shed. Shadows and reflections are all I can see. I'm alone. I take down the metal box next to the rifle and open it.

In my entire life, I've only prayed twice. The first time I prayed that she'd get better; the second, that she would die. Because I needed someone to blame and couldn't find anyone handy. Maybe it was God's fault. I must have pissed him off.

That's what people must need to believe, to have a scapegoat when there's no one left to blame. It's not even a matter of hope, it's about violence.

Tonight I'm not going to pray. Tonight I'm going to go home, kiss Marie, and dream of her, our little girl, the person she was, the swing set, winter.

I empty out the metal box. There are a few cartridges inside. A pouch of tobacco. Wet matches. A piece of paper folded in two that I unfold in the moonlight. 'Dear kids, I went to a concert tonight with your mom. I want you to know that … '

That's where it ends. Nothing further; no signature.

＜

Simon hasn't come home, but I think I heard footsteps in the back alley. Fisher has finished putting in the water heater and closed the wooden door. He tried to gather up his empties but he's too drunk. I help him.

'You're … nice!'

'Yeah.'

'No, I mean it! You're a nice girl. You're polite. You help people. And you stood around listening to me talk shit all day. You're like, perfect. A regular Little Miss Perfect.'

My thoughts turn to what the grocer said. Part of me doesn't want to know why Fisher hates the old guy. But I know I'll be powerless to resist the temptation to ask him sooner or later.

'Did you know the old guy well?'

'Yup.'

'Like him?'

'Yup.'

'Really? Because the grocery store owner told me you didn't like him ... '

'That's none of his business. Of course I liked the old guy. Hate him now, but I liked him before.'

'Why do you hate him?'

Now Fisher's getting mad. He's slurring and his hands are closing up into fists.

'I'm done here. I'm going home.'

'Thanks for the tank, Fisher. What do I owe you?'

'Nothing. Don't owe me nothing. Unless you want to give me a ... Just kidding. Joke.'

'No.'

He lays his hand on my shoulder, as if I were his childhood friend, or a mechanic buddy, or a one-night stand. 'You sure? I did something for you, right?'

He points at the water heater. I take a step back. He takes a step forward.

'I'll pay you for that,' I say. 'How much? Twenty bucks okay?'

He's furious as he grabs me by the shoulder.

'I don't want your money. I want you. Touch me.' He gropes my left breast with his right hand, slides his left between my legs and pushes me against the wall. I make a fist and hit him full-force in the abdomen. He coughs and backs off, and holds himself up on the kitchen table. With his hands palm-down on the table and his neck twisted down toward the ground, he breaks into tears, like a child whose parent said no or took away his toy. He squats down and lays his hand on the wet floor. I wait. The interval between sobs grows longer, as my breathing and heartbeat and the wheezing in my lungs all slow down to normal.

'I didn't want to. Sorry.'

'Get out of here, Fisher. And don't come back.'

'I'm sorry. I just … like to touch.'

He waits for an answer. I don't give him one.

'I just like to touch.'

'Have you touched lots of girls like that? Girls who didn't want you to?'

'Yup.'

'Get out!'

He walks out, his head down. I watch him get into his truck. He starts it, backs up right onto the sidewalk, and peels out like a rapist. I go outside to throw up in the packed-dirt alley. I walk around the house across the yard into the shed. It's pitch black. The darkness makes me feel better.

'Marie?'

'Simon.'

I kiss him like no woman has ever kissed a man, and he holds me like no man has ever held a woman. We're all alone and there's nothing else to do. I won't tell him everything that happened. And he won't tell me all about his evening either. We'll go to sleep in silence and dream of the only person who could make our lives whole again, the one who is dead, the one whose ashes rest in a cardboard box next to the Christmas decorations.

❧

We went back to our chaise longues in the backyard. She went back to occupying every inch of our mental space. The morning is cloudless.

She's not only water; she's also wind and leaves and sunlight. She is nature, all of creation down to the roots that never die.

She's a fox, and a coyote. A swarm of ants a million strong. She's the clouds and the treetops, at the same time, and the fire that razes entire villages.

Even today, we cannot speak her name. Even today, the slightest vibration is enough to unleash in us a pain as powerful as every star in the sky exploding in unison. We'll feel pain in the blood in our veins, but we'll survive.

'I feel like a big breakfast,' Simon says.

'We're out of eggs.'

'I'll go get some.'

'The grocery store's closed.'

'I'll go a little farther.'

Simon gets up and slides his fingers onto my shoulder. I won't do a thing, not one single thing, while I'm waiting for him. I hear the car engine. Gravel crushed under tires. Rubber on asphalt. Silence.

A few minutes later, the same sound of gravel under car tires. Simon must have forgotten something. I hear footsteps, and the back door opens. It isn't Simon. It's Fisher. I immediately sit up straight. The gun is in the shed, but the shed is far away, and I've never handled a gun in my life.

'Don't worry, Marie, I'm not going to do anything. I came to explain.'

'I'd rather not.'

'Just let me explain. You don't have to say a word. And I'll leave right after. But at least I'll know that you know everything.'

I lower my eyes. He sits down next to me, on Simon's chair. He coughs.

'I want to tell you about the day they put in the antenna. It was cold, and they came in with their hard hats and diggers, blueprints and trailers. They cut right through the woods, as if there was nothing there. The forest closed up around them. To forget. They put it in in a single day. The whole village came out to watch. We didn't know what it was we were watching, but we were hypnotized. It was like watching a doctor plunge a needle into a heart, but we weren't in pain. Everything was going fine, even if we had no idea yet that the antenna was only the beginning, that there'd be others. And when one of us left, they'd just come in and put in more antennas, till all that was left was a town full of metal towers. We weren't mad. Just a little sad, I guess.'

As he tells his story, Fisher looks me square in the eye. I massage my right temple with my index finger. He goes on.

'I came out to watch, same as everyone else. With my wife. We didn't bring our son, though. Figured it might be too dangerous. We didn't know about it yet, about the waves and everything. So we asked my sister to look after our son. She wasn't interested in the new antenna. I'm not sure if you know my sister, Alice. The one who doesn't talk. Anyway, when she was babysitting my son, he fell off a slide in the park and broke his neck. The whole town blamed my sister. My wife just blamed me. She moved to the city with my son, where he could get the care he needed. They got a special centre there, for handicapped kids. I wanted to go with them, but my wife didn't want to have anything to do with me. I tried, but every time I went to visit, it only made things worse. It got so going to see my son did more harm than good. And my wife managed to convince me it'd be better for him if I just disappeared. So I came back here, to my hometown, and hid behind a bottle. Lots of bottles. And under cars too. And when I drink, I do bad things. Like yesterday. So you want to know why I hate the old guy? He's my dad. And after everything I went through, I needed my dad to be there for me. And he just lost it, left me for dead. And I hate him for that. But I spent my whole life loving him. Right here in this house, our house. Okay, I'm going now. I won't bother you again. I just wanted you to know.'

I shut my mouth. Fisher stands up without looking at me and goes into the house, walks right through it, gets in his truck, and starts the engine.

Every town has its stories. Dark secrets, accidents, disappearances. I don't believe in destiny, and I'm sure if we landed somewhere else we would have ended up with a bunch of similar horror stories. Every little town has the same stories, and they're always a lot like our own. We chose this house, we chose to be here, to be far away from our old house. As if distance could change anything. We were wrong, of course. For starters, we chose the wrong spot. Our wounds could never heal here, with a child or without. But we'll abide in sorrow, just like Fisher, just like everyone else here.

❧

Simon came home with a dozen eggs, but we decided to go out for breakfast anyway. Maybe we were recreating our first day in town, as if we knew it would be our last.

As we walked, I told Simon the whole story. Fisher and the bracelet and the water heater and the old guy and his son with a broken neck. He told me about Alice, her exile, the antenna. We both made a promise never to lie to each other again, and we both knew we wouldn't keep it.

There on the sidewalk, as a shroud of cloud cover rose up from the forest and the smell of rain suffused the air, we told each other all our deepest, darkest fears. After all these years, it was time. There was the fear of never healing, never finding a way to be happier in this life, never managing to forget. The fear of not being able to break up because of everything we'd been through together, especially after. We'd both be long dead if we weren't there to support each other. We both knew that already, but it still felt good to say it aloud.

We were getting close to the restaurant. Of course, we'd never taste Anne-Benedict's French toast now. But of all the countless things we'd never get to do, it seemed like the least of our concerns. The Lavoies would keep summering here for the next forty years, maybe wondering how they managed to do such a great job of screwing everything up, of striving to be the perfect family for an audience of no one, because the town will have long ceased to exist. Their house will be all that remains, if it doesn't get swallowed up by the mountain. Their house and their freezing-cold swimming pool.

Two drops of rain, one for each of us, fall from the blue sky and graze our cheeks. 'Sexiest Waitresses,' the sign says. Across the street at gas station, Fisher waves just like he did the first day; the bulldozers that will tear down his garage will take him down with them, and he won't mind a bit.

Inside, the burgundy leatherette seats crinkle under our asses, and when Madeleine hands us menus, we're amazed to see her smile. We're the only ones in the dining room, again, at ten a.m. on a Tuesday. Everyone must be working, or sleeping, or just driving by; or maybe they have simply ceased to exist. That must be it, they've just ceased to exist.

'How's it going, lovebirds?'

'It's going.'

'Nice cup of coffee?'

'Please. And orange juice.'

We'll never see those orange juices, any more than we did the first time. Madeleine will serve us the same thing, the same bad eggs and coffees filled up to the brims. She'll be less cheerful, but she'll still charge us for the Wednesday Special.

'So you know everything now?'

'Yup.'

'And I warned you that it was none of your business, right?'

'Yeah. You were right.'

'There's no point dredging up the past. Not here. Here, every time someone starts messing with the past, we lose another bunch of people. They go to the city, or they move to the forest. We never see them again.'

'Can I ask you a question? The old guy. What did he do for a living?'

'The old guy who lived in your house? He wasn't from here. He was some university guy, from the city. But one day he fell in love with a girl from here. Prettiest girl in town. No genius, but he liked her anyway. She looked just like Alice: they were dead ringers. But he was always real busy, the old guy. Head in a book, or in his music scores. He was a musician. One of the greats, they said. They say he wrote beautiful music. That's what they say, at least. I couldn't really tell you.'

'He was a composer?'

'Yeah. But I wouldn't know anything about that.'

'How'd he die?'

'I don't know. Everyone around here just figures he let himself die of a broken heart.'

'Yeah, that must be it.'

'But they never found his body. There was a pool of blood in the shed, but no body. We threw a little sand and some rocks over the dirt floor. And just figured he died of sorrow. Worked for us.'

Madeleine wiped her eyes with her apron.

~

Fall is in the air and, out here in the country, the days are getting cooler. On the sidewalk Marie's progress has slowed almost to a standstill, as if she knows that once we go inside we'll never leave the house again. The air is fresh.

We inch along at a snail's pace and soon we're walking by the park and can't help shivering at the sight of the slide. Forty years from now, this park will be gone as well, and nothing will be left to preserve the memory of the accident that broke the whole town's heart. Marie takes me by the hand.

'Sure is a cute town,' she says. 'We picked a winner.'

'Yeah.'

'What's your favourite memory here?'

I should perhaps have kept it to myself, but it seems like we're long past lying to save face. I tell her about the bowling alley, describe the people and the sounds and the sense of joy. Hot dogs and bowling shoes, the kid with different-coloured eyes, the blaring music. I tell her how good I felt that day, and that long drawn-out moment when I could finally feel my heart beating normally, without clenching up.

'Marguerite was there too. She was bowling. And laughing. Remember her laugh? She was laughing, and it wasn't even painful to me.'

'Take me there.'

~

We cut through the backyard and into the forest, leaving a few drops of our blood on the branches. I followed Simon for hours, as we walked on a carpet of pine needles and leaves. We crossed the river with no current. We saw the fox, and the coyote, and wept together in the stillness when we saw the singing birds, though we still couldn't hear their song. We went looking for Simon's bowling alley. Out of the corner of my eye, between two tree trunks, I thought I saw my parents' restaurant, but when I turned around it was gone.

After what seemed like a thousand kilometres, we reached the antenna. Without a word, we both crawled under the fence. Simon leaned against a steel post. For a second I fought for breath. I felt a force pushing down on my lungs, and I felt a sweet drowning, an attraction. When I put my hand on the antenna, I took in so much oxygen, flowing in so fast it choked me and, in a moment of clarity, I saw everything. The future awaiting the four of us. The peace we'd know at last. I closed my eyes and held Simon tight. The vibrating antenna was the only music we needed to cradle each other.

There was no other child like our daughter. Those black eyes and those thousand and one lives she'd lived before she joined us in this one, her skin pale like the wind. She was our life, a tiny giantess we endlessly searched for. For three years we have walked down the road that led us here, to this antenna that casts a crushing shadow over an entire town. This small, languishing town, dying one family at a time.

In the forest, with its floor of crumpled leaves, Alice appears out of nowhere with her barbed-wire eyes and determined walk.

She says hi, as if she'd always known she'd find us here. Though we didn't see her duck under the fence, and now she's next to us. She turns to me and speaks.

'You know I can talk, right?'

'Yeah.'

'So from now on I'm going to talk. To everyone. I haven't done anything wrong. I shouldn't have hidden. I shouldn't have believed them. I believed them, and that's my fault. But what happened wasn't my fault.'

'It wasn't your fault.'

'I would have liked the chance to mourn my father. I left just before he died. And I knew he was going to die.'

'What do you mean?'

'He'd gone out for a walk in the forest. He told me the story while I was packing my bags. He'd seen something over across the river. A concert hall. Full of people, all kinds of people, from all over. There were people he recognized from around town, and others he'd never seen before. But the main thing was he was sure he saw my mother. She'd aged, but he was sure it was her. And my brother's son too. And he told me he was going to join them. By that point he was getting senile, not always talking sense. And I left. I didn't stay to help him. That's why I came back. Because I never should have left without him.'

Simon leapt up. He was agitated.

'Your dad,' he said. 'Did your dad wear a tuxedo when he performed? Was he a big guy? With a loud laugh?'

'Yeah, why?'

'And your brother's son … did he have different-coloured eyes? One brown and one blue?'

'How'd you know that?'

～

The concert hall, the bowling alley, my parents' restaurant – all of it exists. It has to. If the old guy could go and find the ones who've disappeared, we too can go and find our daughter. I squeeze Simon's arm.

'We have to go.'

The gun has waited for us in the shed. I lug my cello down to the kitchen, so I can bring it with me. Finger on the trigger. One shot, then another. On this day in September 1977, we left to join our daughter at the end of the road, in a dying town covered in scarlet scars.

Forty years from now, no one will remember us.

～

Our bodies are never found. Just the blood on the floor. Fisher will say he never saw it coming. The Lavoies will say we were 'such nice people.' Alice won't say a thing, and the blood will dry between the old planks of the hundred-year-old house we left behind.

～

In the distance, a bird sings in the rain.

Matthieu Simard is the author of eight novels. He has been called one of the most promising Québécois authors of his generation.

Pablo Strauss grew up in British Columbia and now makes his home in Quebec City. He has translated several works of fiction from Quebec, including David Turgeon's *The Supreme Orchestra* and Maxime Raymond Bock's *Baloney*.

Typeset in Albertina

Printed at the Coach House on bpNichol Lane in Toronto, Ontario, on Zephyr Antique Laid paper, which was manufactured, acid-free, in Saint-Jérôme, Quebec, from second-growth forests. This book was printed with vegetable-based ink on a 1973 Heidelberg KORD offset litho press. Its pages were folded on a Baumfolder, gathered by hand, bound on a Sulby Auto-Minabinda and trimmed on a Polar single-knife cutter.

Translated by Pablo Strauss
Edited by Alana Wilcox
Cover design by Ingrid Paulson
Design by Crystal Sikma
Author photo by Idra Labrie
Translator photo by Étienne Dionne

Coach House Books
80 bpNichol Lane
Toronto ON M5S 3J4
Canada

416 979 2217
800 367 6360

mail@chbooks.com
www.chbooks.com